Michael J. Stishl

SANCTUARY

BLACK HARE PRESS SHORT READS

WARDENCLYFFE by GREGG CUNNINGHAM

HADES 11 by PAUL WARMERDAM

BLOOD AND SILK by ZOEY XOLTON

AS ABOVE, SO BENEATH by JOSHUA D. TAYLOR

THE RISE OF THE GREAT OLD ONE by JASMINE JARVIS

CHRYSALIS by KIMBERLY REI

MOUNT TERROR by E.L. GILES

THE RECKONING by STEPHANIE SCISSOM

THE SPIRIT OF RODEO by BETH W. PATTERSON

CARPE DETRITUS by TIM MENDEES

THE BOOKWORM by L.T. EMERY & ANDREAS HORT

THE SALAMANDRION by MIKE ADAMSON

THIS HIDEOUS JOY by JONATHAN INBODY

THE CORONER by J. MOTOKI

FINGERPRINT FORENSICS SHORT READS

DEAD MAN WALKING by DAVID GREEN
MR HANGMAN by SCOTT MCGREGOR

⬤

HELL HARE HOUSE SHORT READS

SEEING by PATRICK WINTERS
RAINMAKER by BILL HUGHES
TESATO'S CODE by KAREN BAYLY
THE PUB AT CROKERS CROSSING by KRIS ASHTON
THE DEVIL AND THE LOCH ARD GORGE by LEANBH PEARSON
SANCTUARY by MICHAEL J. STIEHL
CLOWN DIARY – APPENDIX 7 by JOE OPPENHEIMER

Contents

Chapter One

heobard awoke to the sound of his door lock clacking open. It ricocheted off the stone walls of his chamber, forcing the fog of sleep from his mind. He focused on the thick wooden door that separated his room from the adjoining hall and felt an acute dread of the unknown.

"Who's there?" he called, struggling to untangle himself from his thin cotton blanket. He had twisted it around himself as protection against a cool breeze that had oozed through his window and crawled over his body as he slept. A metal grate covered the window, carving the moonlight that spilled through it into pieces and casting it as distended, pale blue squares across the floor. He fumbled to his feet and stood among the pattern of light and dark, the blanket remaining stubbornly wrapped around his legs.

The door burst open, and Dak entered the room. Framed by the inky black hallway and illuminated by a single candle he held in a worn metal holder, his thick, black monastic robes made his head look as though it were floating disembodied in the night. As his broad, hulking figure marched across the room, the warm corona of light that seeped from his candle engulfed Theobard.

Dak arched the thick, dark eyebrows that floated just below the severe bangs of his short-cropped brown hair and twisted his mouth into a disapproving shape. Through a small gap in the high, stiff, black, collar that surrounded his neck, Theobard saw a two-inch vertical scar on his throat. Holding his right hand near the candle flame, Dak began moving his long, rough fingers.

Have sinned, he signed. *Must atone.*

He waited for the required response.

Through blood, my sin is washed away. Through blood, my spirit is clean. For Bulahl, I am made silent and will raise my voice no more, Theobard signed back, cursing himself for his lapse.

He held out his hands, palms down, and Dak struck them five times with a length of loose leather cord that dangled from a knot on his belt. Blood welled out of the wounds and ran over the back of his hands. Staring down, Theobard realised he had lost count of the scars.

Dak moved to the centre of the cell and placed the candleholder on a small, crudely made wooden table. The table and a matching chair were the only other pieces of furniture in the room besides Theobard's bunk. The light from the candle provided dim but sufficient light by which to communicate, and Theobard wondered if the challenge of signing by candlelight was one of the reasons the Silent Brotherhood remained in their cells at night.

Dak walked forwards and smiled. He grabbed the blanket tangled around Theobard and carefully unwound it. When finished, he looked at Theobard with a smile and signed, *Defeated by a blanket.*

It is a wily foe, Theobard replied, his gap-toothed grin wide and genuine.

Hurry, get dressed, Dak signed with urgency, his face serious. *We are needed at the gate.*

In the more than ten years he had lived with the Silent Brothers, Theobard had never been needed at the gate. Not once. Not ever. Numb, he did as Dak instructed and got dressed. *What's wrong?* he signed impulsively before pulling on the tan linen pants, off-white tunic, and boiled leather sandals all initiates wore.

There has been an accident, Dak replied, holding his hands near the candle. *The gate portcullis is jammed. Brother Balcus and Brother Marco are outside of the wall with a newly arrived caravan.*

Dak need say nothing else. Brother Balcus and Brother Marco were dim, lazy, and mean. Many in the Brotherhood disliked them, and it was no accident they had been assigned to the main gate overnight. It was the kind of place they could do the least amount of harm.

Dak grabbed the candle and began walking back across the room, towards the dark hallway. Once Theobard caught up, he thrust his hands into the light of the flickering candle and signed, *Why is there a caravan at night?*

Don't know, Dak replied, moving the candleholder higher up, and further out, in front of him to signal the end of the conversation.

Theobard nearly blurted out the question foremost in his mind, but caught himself. *No one travels through the Dogyari in the dark,* he thought. *What could be so important that a caravan would come now?* Theobard supposed he would know the answer soon enough.

Once outside of his cell, they walked briskly around the curving balcony that formed the main passageway of the dormitory. As they moved past a pair of Brothers holding the curved ceremonial swords of the night patrol, Theobard nodded and signed, *Good Morning.* They replied with a curt nod.

The dormitory was crescent-shaped and two stories high. Its back merged with the great curving wall of the sanctuary and its front formed a semi-circle around the temple, which was a tall, round stone tower with a wide square base in which was set a large arching entryway. At the top of the temple was the Eye of Bulahl, a single bright light that shone down upon the sanctuary. Tonight, the light was golden; Bulahl was pleased.

They descended a set of stairs at the end of the balcony and turned right to cross the great cobblestone courtyard that separated the dormitory from the temple. To his right, Theobard saw the smithy where Brother Tanner clanged away each day, making and repairing their metal goods. On the side of the smithy closest to the main gate, which sat directly on the opposite side of the temple from the dormitory, towered a large, broken water clock, its hands frozen in place. Theobard had never learned to tell time, but enjoyed staring at the clock's looming geometric face. He often wondered what had been happening at the sanctuary the moment those hands had frozen.

To his left, beyond the soaring temple, was the stable and storehouse. They, too, backed up to the great stone wall that encircled the sanctuary. The Brothers owned precious few livestock, so the stables were mostly empty.

The storehouse was another matter. Brother Strunk kept it well stocked and efficiently run. Dak had once told Theobard of the many wise decisions Abbott Emerlich had made as leader of the Brotherhood putting a fat glutton of a monk in charge of the storehouse was one of his best.

Moonlight poured into the courtyard and Theobard thought how funny it looked to see it empty. Most days, the Brothers swirled around it, busy with the tasks they were given by Dak or one of the other senior Brothers. He missed the sound of their feet padding on the bricks, the casual greetings they gave one another as they passed, and the gentile smiles that graced their faces as they worked.

He looked toward the gigantic main gate of the sanctuary and saw that it was robed in wisps of early morning fog. The same cool breeze that had slunk into his cell spun the fog away then, carrying it along in swirling, ghostly shapes. Theobard knew it would melt away as soon as the hot sun crawled its way above the looming wall. He looked forward to that radiating heat and imagined its comforting warmth as he carted supplies or patched broken bricks in the courtyard later that morning.

On either side of the gate were bundles of torches, their flames vainly leaping at the departing mist. The wall that curved around the perimeter of the sanctuary was composed of an amalgam of stones of varying sizes and shapes, some as large as twenty feet across, and others hardly larger than a pebble. An ancient mortar, endlessly patched by the Brotherhood, held it together. No one knew how old the wall was, or who had built it, only that it was a perfect circle and that it must never be allowed to fall into disrepair.

Even the stone that had been used to build it was a mystery, since the sanctuary was surrounded by a vast stretch of swamp, marshland, and soft-bottomed shallow rivers known as the Dogyari. The Dogyari was a treacherous place, even during the day and in the best of weather. Full of quicksand, prone to water washing away well-worn paths by endlessly swelling and receding, and full of thick tangles of dense shrubs, it was a place only the skilled could navigate safely. *To cross it on a night like this*, Theobard thought to himself, *would be suicidal.*

Once in front of the ornate gate, Theobard instantly understood the problem. The portcullis hung two feet off the ground. The clever mechanism that caused a geometric pattern of squares to shift into circles as it lifted was jammed, leaving the shapes frozen in mid-transformation.

Without breaking his stride, Dak nimbly crawled under the gate, no small feat for a man of his bulk. Theobard stopped and stared at it. He fumbled with his fingers for a moment, then tugged nervously at the cuffs of his tunic.

He had not been through the gate since he had arrived at the Sanctuary. He had been only eight or nine—his parents had never celebrated his birthday, so he wasn't sure. He could see the fear on his father's face when, red eyed and crying, Theobard had reached for him. He remembered the look of disgust that twisted his father's mouth just before he growled the word "devil" and walked away.

Theobard touched the gate and then the wall. The feeling of the cold metal and rough stone soothed him. He couldn't help but think that he was being a fool for leaving the safety of the Sanctuary, even if only for a short while. He forced that thought from his mind, placed his faith in Dak and Bulahl, and plunged ahead.

Chapter Two

The girl with the bronze skin was laughing. She sat on the back of a careworn old mule not far from where Dak and Theobard struggled with the portcullis. "You'll snap yourself in half before you lift that," she said, her cheerful voice smoothing a sarcastic tone.

Dak and Theobard gave the portcullis another heave, pointedly ignoring her. It did not budge. Defeated, they turned their backs to it, slumped to the ground, and rested against the cool, rough stones of the Sanctuary's wall. The great gate soared over their heads; its smooth finished stones locked together in a crisp geometric pattern that contrasted with the geologic chaos of the wall that supported it. The broken portcullis appeared to Theobard like the teeth of a great laughing face.

Theobard watched the slow-moving water of the indolent river surrounding the Sanctuary pass under the sturdy bridge that connected them to the mainland. Its gentle burbling against bridge pilings created a soothing murmur. Theobard found it comforting to see with his own eyes something he had heard so many nights in his cell.

"We need to try something else." Dak signed to Theobard.

Theobard agreed, but didn't know what. He stared at the girl, who was absently swinging her feet back and forth along the sides of the mule. She met his gaze with a fierce look and a half smile, which Theobard found unsettling. He was not bothered because she was a girl—something that was forbidden in the Sanctuary. He was bothered because she was entirely too carefree for someone strapped to a pack animal with her hands tied.

She continued to defy his stare even as a curtain of her long, black, tightly curled hair slowly slipped across her face, covering half of it completely. Light from the torches on either side of the gate reflected off her single visible eye and Theobard struggled to place its colour, ultimately deciding that it looked metallic and golden. She continued to stare, her strange eye daring him to look away. He did.

If only Brother Balcus and Brother Marco weren't so difficult, he thought, *or so foolish as to have insulted and injured the caravan traders.*

Theobard thought back to the confusing scene confronting him once he had gathered the courage to crawl under the portcullis after Dak. In the dim moonlight that filtered through the fog, they had seen two traders; one older, one younger, arguing with Balcus and Marco.

Theobard had been shocked to see the two Brothers openly yelling at the traders, the light from their torches flickering across their contorted faces. Dak, seeing his concern, signed to him that outside of the wall, it was not a sin to speak. This had calmed Theobard some, but he still feared the consequences, despite Dak's assurance.

Dak had taken charge of the scene, intervening with a few furious signs that Balcus translated for the befuddled traders. Peace followed his insistence that Balcus and Marco apologise for whatever offence they had caused. Feet shuffling, eyes to the ground, they did as they were told.

Theobard's muscles ached as he sat looking at the trader's creaky, old, covered wagon. He was still angry Marco and Balcus had contrived inventorying it to avoid helping with the portcullis. It was a worn old thing, its wooden wheels cracked and chipped from many trips down bumpy roads, with crude patches strewn across its canvas covering. Harnessed to its front were two ancient nags that looked to have seen as many miles as the wagon they pulled.

The older of the two traders stood next to the wagon dressed in the fancifully coloured breeches of the Duarbu. He wore a matching blouse, covered in mud, and was holding his right arm with his left, in obvious pain. Next to him stood a younger trader, who Theobard assumed was his son. They shared the same hawkish nose and beady eyes, but the lad was taller than his father and skinnier, with a drawn and bony face giving him the impression of one who had experience going without food.

Theobard noticed the younger man scowling at him, words soundlessly forming on his lips as though he were practicing a speech. He had blood running down the bridge of his nose and Theobard watched as the lad carelessly rubbed the beige sleeve of his shirt across his face. The older man's enormous eyebrows were furrowed in pain above his eyes, like two caterpillars mating. Theobard saw mud crusted in his long drooping moustache and wondered if the man had fallen on his face.

"Oafs!" the lad yelled in a reedy voice, startling Balcus and Marco as they pretended to count items in the wagon. "My father's head coulda been caved in by ya thick skulls. Hadn't no one told you never ta grab another man's horse?"

The words echoed briefly off the towering stone walls and across the vastness of the Dogyari. Neither Balcus nor Marco replied, which only angered the young trader further. "Stop ya stallin' now and pay up! We brung what ya asked for, and then some. Lucky we don't charge ya more for the insult."

"How was I supposed to know that sack of bones was so skittish?" Balcus roared. "If you'd helped us unload the cart, as I asked, there would have been no need for me to come near that old nag, let alone drag her toward the gate."

"We're traders, not porters," the old man croaked. "Even without this,"—he indicated his right arm—"no way we was ever gonna haul this stuff under ya broken down old gate. That, brother, is ya own business."

Dak got to his feet with a sigh and headed toward the four of them. Theobard began to follow, but Dak signed for him to stay put. Theobard obeyed.

"Just pay us already and we'll unload this stuff right here. We're eager to be rid of ya," barked the young trader. "I couldn't care less if tha Devil himself took it now, so long as we get our coin."

Dak touched Balcus on the shoulder and signed to him so quickly Theobard couldn't follow. Balcus made a questioning face and replied with a short burst of signs. Theobard saw Dak give the unmistakable sign for "Go!" and Balcus slunk off towards the gate, eventually disappearing under the broken portcullis.

"Hey," said the girl on the mule, "do you understand what I'm saying?"

Theobard nodded that he did.

"Good, come here."

Theobard stood and walked closer. He saw she was about his age, maybe a little older. Under her unruly hair, Theobard could see her pert nose and large, round eyes sat on a beautifully oval face. His eyes drifted reflexively downward to the ground. As they did, he took note of her loose fitting indigo short-sleeved blouse, riddled with a yellow undulating pattern, which elegantly displayed her supple yet well-muscled arms. She wore a pair of leather riding pants that hugged the shape of her graceful legs, tucked neatly into a pair of knee-high, black boots. The boots had the image of a well-muscled man breaking a chain under a rising sun worked into them with raised golden thread. It was beautiful, and Theobard reached out to run his fingers along the pattern.

"What are you doing?" said the girl, moving her foot away from him. "Eyes here," she ordered, to bring his attention back to her face.

Sorry, Theobard signed.

"Are you mute?" she asked.

Theobard struggled to answer. He was afraid of his voice. He knew Dak had said it wasn't a sin to speak outside of the wall, but it wasn't Dak's wrath he feared. He looked at the girl and saw her boiling impatience, watched her cross her arms and glare at him. He felt the pressure of her expectation and his need to please her collide.

"No," he whispered, shaking his head from side to side.

"Good," she replied. "That will make this easier. I can fix it."

Theobard looked at her, confusion spreading across his face.

"Your portcullis—your gate—I can fix what's wrong with it."

"You can?" he ventured quietly, feeling reassured there had been no consequence following his last response.

"Yes, I gather that's the source of the problem here, isn't it? I mean, aside from four lazy men who don't want to do a damn bit of work."

"I suppose," Theobard stammered, remembering he was prone to doing that.

"With the gate fixed, they can pull that wagon inside, unload it, and be on their way. I'm tired of sitting here. I'd rather be back trudging through the swamp with those two idiots than listening to another minute of this stupid argument."

"Ok," Theobard mumbled. "I'll tell them."

"Good," replied the girl, pushing her hair out of her face with her bound hands. "And make sure you tell them I can't fix anything all tied up."

As Theobard turned to walk towards Dak, he saw Brother Balcus return. He had just finished crawling under the gate and was beginning to stand. Once Balcus was fully upright, Theobard noticed a glazed pot with the picture of a dragonfly impressed into its side at his feet. Balcus stooped down, picked up the pot and carried it towards where Dak, Marco, and the two traders were standing. Theobard broke into a trot to catch up with Balcus, curious as to what he had brought.

"That seems fair," Theobard heard the older trader say to Dak once he got closer. "But yer takin' the girl. You never said nothin' 'bout wanting only boys. Orphans only was what ya said. We're out a good bit for draggin' her 'cross this swamp."

"That's your problem," blurted Marco. "We don't pay for Duarbu ignorance or orphan girls we can't understand."

The younger trader's face flushed, and he appeared on the verge of shouting something when Dak's hands clapped together like thunder. Everyone stood in silence as he locked Marco in a withering glare. He signed that Marco should go back inside the Sanctuary. Reluctantly, Marco complied, slinking off toward the gate.

Theobard saw his chance and tugged on Dak's sleeve. *The girl says she can help*, he signed.

How? Dak replied, confused.

She says she can fix the portcullis.

You understand her? Dak replied, confusion wiping away the frustration that had been lodged on his face.

"What's he sayin'?" demanded the old trader. "Come, come, no secrets."

Theobard looked at Dak, who indicated it was okay for him to respond.

"The girl…" Theobard began, unconsciously tugging at the collar of his tunic.

"Speak up!" crowed the old man. "These worn-out ears can't hear ya."

"The girl," Theobard repeated louder, rocking back and forth slightly on his feet. "The one you brought. She says can fix our gate."

"Does she now?" said the younger trader. "And ya actually understand the gibberish comin' out her mouth?"

"Yes," said Theobard, confused. "She said if you untie her, she'll fix the gate so we can bring the supplies inside, where it would be easier to unload them."

"Well, I don't know nothin' 'bout that," said the younger man. "All the way here she just kept yappin' 'bout the same thing to us, over and over. Complete gobbledygook. Got right mad at us for ignoring her, actually."

"Clobbered me with a log when I wasn't lookin'," grumbled the old trader, rubbing his head at the memory. "Plannin' to run's my guess. That's why we tied her up. She'll do the same to you, if'n ya don't watch out."

Dak looked thoughtful for a moment and then signed something to Balcus. Balcus handed him the jar, before turning to speak to the old trader. "Brother Dak has asked that you roll up your sleeve," he said, pointing at the trader's injured arm, "so that he, with the help of the mighty Bulahl, may heal it."

The old trader was suspicious but, seized by another wave of pain, gingerly rolled back his sleeve. He revealed an open, seeping wound, deep bruising, and an arm that was no longer straight. Dak removed the lid from the jar and placed it in the pocket of his robe. He jabbed two fingers into the jar and pulled out a thick, viscous, light green fluid that smelled of swamp.

Dak smeared the substance liberally over the trader's arm, rinsing off what remained on his hand in a nearby puddle. Then he removed the lid from his pocket, placed it back on the jar, and handed it to Balcus. Theobard watched in amazement as the trader's arm straightened, the wound closed, and the bruising disappeared. Relief swept across the old man's face.

"By all tha's holy…" the old man said with wonder as he examined his arm.

Dak handed the younger trader the jar and then signed, *Take as our apology. A gift from mighty Bulahl,* which Balcus begrudgingly repeated out loud.

Dak removed a three-inch-long knife from the pocket of his robe. He gave it to Theobard and signed, *Free the girl and fix the portcullis.*

Theobard held the knife with care and hurried over to the girl. As he approached, she held out her bound wrists and said, "Glad to see someone around here has some sense."

Theobard cut her free. She untied the rope binding her to the saddle and leapt from the back of the mule to the ground. She pushed her hair out of her face and leered with her golden eyes past Theobard. Curious, he looked back to where Dak stood and saw everyone staring at them.

A brisk wind began to blow from deep within the Dogyari. It moved through the moss hanging in the trees, and over the still and stagnant waters, until it parted the swirling fog. Moonlight glinted off the metal portcullis and he saw the girl's eyes drawn to its complex pattern of curved and straight interlocking metal pieces.

"It's beautiful," she said with awe. "These shapes change when the gate is opened or closed, right?"

"Yes," replied Theobard, impressed by her perception.

She took a few strides towards it, ignoring Theobard, and cast her eyes downwards. She snatched a small, straight stick from the ground as Theobard followed her. Once in front of the portcullis, she slowly rubbed her hand across its surface, feeling its texture. "A Katuri mechanism," she said, turning to Theobard. "These are rare. It's sad no one has maintained it."

Theobard found himself drawn to her face. To her full, pouting lips and her thin, questioning eyebrows. But most of all to her golden eyes that flashed whenever moonlight or torchlight collided with them. He wondered what her cascading black hair felt like. What it smelled like.

"What's a katuri?" he said.

"Not a *what*," she replied, her hand absently searching across the metal frame holding the portcullis to the smooth stones of the gate. "A *who*. Katuri was the youngest son of the famous clockmaker, Mosutaga. As a child, he became obsessed with the gears and mechanisms of his father's clocks, grew up building them. He became convinced that mechanisms could improve anything. Spent his life building them into all sorts of objects."

Her hands continued to search the edge of the portcullis, gently caressing its curving form. "The thing about this style of portcullis," she went on, oblivious to Theobard's unwavering gaze, "is that they are overly reliant on a master coil to aid in lifting the extra bulk caused by the decorative mechanisms."

She stopped moving her hand and looked directly at Theobard. "Knowing that," she continued, "anyone with the skill to build a Katuri gate as beautiful as this would have put a release in it so the coil could be replaced when it wore out."

Without a word, she rolled under the partially open portcullis, skilfully avoiding its hanging spikes. Once on the other side, she stood in a single fluid movement and continued her search.

"Here," she said, jamming the stick into a tiny circular opening half way down outer edge of the gate.

There was a loud click, and after a short pause, the portcullis crashed to the ground.

"Oh great!" roared Balcus, raising his hands in the air. "She broke it!"

"What's he barking about?" said the girl, jabbing the stick in Balcus's direction.

"He thinks you've broken it."

"He's quite dim, isn't he?" she said with a grin, and Theobard couldn't help smiling.

"Help me," she said, indicating Theobard should lift the gate with her.

He moved closer, placing his hands at the bottom of the portcullis. "Don't worry," she said in a comforting tone, "you were fighting against the mechanism before. It should be easier now."

Theobard's hand brushed against the girl's as he prepared to lift, the warmth of it thrilling. "It's a shame you won't see these shapes do their dance with the coil removed," she said, beginning to lift, "but we'd best open this before your friend turns purple."

Theobard felt the portcullis give. It was heavy, but together they were moving it. He stole a quick glance at the girl's well-muscled arms as they pulled it upward and felt guilty. After a few moments, they had it above their heads. "Just one more shove," she said, "and a safety mechanism should lock into place."

As they stood frozen, both preparing for one final heave, Theobard became aware they were only inches apart, nearly pressed together, staring into each other's eyes.

"Now," she said, and together they shifted the great metal portcullis upwards until they heard a loud click.

The girl let go of the portcullis and stood back, looking triumphant. Theobard unclasped his hands slowly, half expected it to fall down.

"We did it." Theobard said staring in awe up at the portcullis.

"We sure did. My name is Dellia, by the way," she said, holding out her hand.

"Theobard," he replied with a gap-toothed grin, grasping her finely shaped fingers in his calloused and dirt-stained hand.

Chapter Three

T o-mor-row." Theobard said, sounding out each part of the word in his head. It was written in chalk on the underside of a brick he had just taken from the stack next to him. He held it in his hand and felt pride at having worked it out himself. After more than three months of memorisation, knowing the alphabet was paying off.

He shovelled a small amount of loose sand from the wheelbarrow on his right into the gap between the bricks in front of him. The bricks of the courtyard were the heart of the Sanctuary because the courtyard was where life in the Brotherhood took place. From daily initiate instruction, to the fall harvest celebration—all the bonds that made them Brothers were formed here.

It was his job to keep it in good repair and he derived great satisfaction and dignity from the task. Each day, he found loose or broken bricks and replaced them—at least, when bricks were available, which was more often now Dellia was around to keep the kiln in good repair.

He turned the brick so that the word "tomorrow" faced down and slotted it into place with care. It was perfectly level, like those on either side of it, and when taken together, the bricks of the courtyard formed a grooved surface of repeating patterns, spinning away from him in every direction for more than two hundred feet. Dak often told him he had the hands of a healer when it came to paving stone. Theobard smiled broadly at the thought of it.

He stood, his knees cracking, and wondered how long he had been at it. He often lost track of time when working. It never much mattered what Dak asked him to do; he always enjoyed it and the contribution it made to the Brotherhood. He laughed to himself when he thought of all the words he'd placed facedown around the courtyard since Dellia had arrived. He wondered if there was some sort of message taking shape out there under everyone's feet. Knowing Dellia, there was.

The words on the bricks had been her idea. She had demanded a way to pay him back for teaching her the Brotherhood's hand signs, and when she'd learned he couldn't read, that had settled it. *Knowing read*, she had signed clumsily to him, *make us not animal*. Theobard insisted he had no use for reading and no debt was owed, but she would have none of it. Like waves lapping the shore, she returned to the topic over and again until he gave in.

Theobard enjoyed tutoring Dellia. She was bright and fearless and picked up the hand signs faster than most. He had been surprised when Dak had chosen him for the task. Typically, such important work would have fallen on a lay brother and not an initiate like him. A lay brother would have incorporated the teachings of Bulahl into each lesson, making sure Dellia learned as much about their God as she did about how to communicate with the Brothers. But Dak had been too busy to do it himself, and the other Brothers had refused to teach a woman, so it had come down to him.

Dak had said it would be a good way to prove himself to the Brotherhood, a crucial thing for an initiate who would soon be petitioning to become a lay brother. Lessons took place outside the Sanctuary walls, allowing the student to remain free from sin as they said their words a final time. A sign mastered meant the student no longer had dominion over that word, and now it belonged to the still water and verdant trees of the Dogyari. At the end of each lesson, both tutor and student gave thanks to Bulahl for the gift of proper speech, and a new life free of blasphemy.

Teaching Dellia reminded Theobard of his own training. He had been a small child, but still recalled with clarity the terror invading him each time he imagined his words leaving him and submerging themselves in the Dogyari forever. In those days, he often dreamt of quicksand and drowning.

Fortunately, Dellia did not feel the same. She would laugh when she mastered a new sign and delighted in sending the old word away. Once, when Theobard had asked her about it, she had signed, *Word will have own adventure now. Others may find. Use for better things than me.*

To Theobard, it was an unusual reaction, but then everything about Dellia was unusual. Women and girls were not allowed in the Sanctuary, and yet here she was. No one knew what language she spoke, but Theobard could understand her nevertheless. The Sanctuary was full of broken, old mechanisms that had confounded even the brightest of the Brothers, however there wasn't one Dellia couldn't fix with enough time and the right tools. All of this made the days since she had arrived special; a remarkable break from the comforting routine that had been Theobard's life.

Dak had understood her value right away, on the very night the Duarbu had brought her. *She's a mechanique,* he'd signed to Theobard after the traders had left. Theobard had not understood the sign, having never seen it before, and it had taken Dak quite some time to explain the concept.

Dellia belonged to a rare group of people who had a gift for mechanical objects. Some speculated that machaniques were themselves, machines—composed of springs and gears under their skin—but Dak thought that idea ridiculous. What set them apart, he explained, was their metallic gold eyes and boundless knowledge of mechanical objects. *All mechaniques have gold eyes,* Dak had said. *It's how you know they're truly gifted and not just clever fakers.*

A loud clack sounded, and Theobard turned his attention to the enormous water clock standing next to the smithy. He was still getting used to the sound of its gears moving, and the hands on its face changing place throughout the day. He was not sure he liked that Dellia had fixed it—he'd enjoyed the rhythm of his days being driven by the Liturgy of Hours, mealtimes, and his regular chore schedule. The mechanical ordering of things did not suit him.

He hurried toward the main gate of the Sanctuary, worried he would be late. Passing through it, he turned left and thought about how common it had become for him to leave its walls. He still felt uneasy being outside of them, but seeing Dellia always banished his fears.

She was waiting for him, looking off into the distance at the House of the Elders with a melancholy look on her face. It was a squat, two story brick building on the opposite side of the meandering river that separated the Sanctuary from the rest of the Dogyari. It was partially obscured by trees, but its pitched red tile roof could just be seen from where they stood.

Her long black, curly hair was pulled back into a ponytail, which, Theobard knew, meant she had just been working. A tool belt hung from her full, curving hips. Each time he saw her, it seemed to acquire some new device he didn't understand. He wondered sometimes what she would do when she ran out of space for new tools on that belt. Get a second one, he supposed.

Theobard stumbled over a root in the path and nearly lost his sandal. "Oh, hello," she said in a subdued voice, turning to stare at him with her large, golden eyes.

In the moment, he found himself struck by her beauty, as he often had been since he'd met her, and was at a loss for words. Fumbling for a response, he watched as Dellia twisted her mouth into an off-centre smile.

I know, she signed, *'Hello' belongs to the Dogyari.*

Yes, he signed back, trying to recover his composure. *Make it practiced, make it perfect. It is a sin to use words that are no longer ours.*

Nearby, a hawk leapt off the gnarled branch of an ancient tree and into the air, its large grey and brown wings outstretched. It soared in a circle above their heads, and they watched it until it dived out of sight.

"They're beautiful, aren't they?" Dellia said, her eyes fixed on where the hawk had been. "So graceful and wild. Sometimes I wish I could fly free like that."

Dellia, Theobard signed with reproach. *Use your signs. We are here to learn.*

"I know enough," she said. "Can't we, just for once, take a break?"

Theobard felt conflicted. He knew his duty was to teach, but the sound of her rich, warm voice tempted him.

"Come on," she continued. "You know Marco and Balcus talk all night long when they're out here. Those two are the worst monks I've ever seen."

She took a step closer to him and gently placed her hand on his arm. "Did you get my message?"

Yes, he signed.

"Out loud…" she coaxed him, her golden eyes filled with mischief.

"Yes," he repeated in a quiet voice.

"That's better," she said, sliding her hand off his arm. "You have a nice voice, you know. It's very sincere and sweet."

"Thank you," he said, feeling awkward.

"So, what was the word? Could you read it?"

"Yes. It was 'tomorrow'," he said, looking around to see if any of the other Brothers were out beyond the wall. Off in the distance was the Sanctuary's small gatehouse, and in it, Theobard could see Brother Maynard. The old monk's eyes were buried under the mounds of wrinkled skin that made up his weathered face, but Theobard had no doubt that they still saw keenly. He turned his back on Maynard and began walking along the wall. Dellia followed.

"Don't worry about old Maynard," she said as they walked. "He lost his key to his cell yesterday. That's the third time this month. Dak would have been furious if he'd found out. I made him a new one, so he owes me. He's actually an old sweetie under all those wrinkles."

Theobard's fingers fumbled over themselves as he struggled to reply without signing. "Why 'tomorrow'?" he said at last.

"Because," she said with a grin. "Did you bring your map?"

"Yes," he replied, catching a glimpse of the hawk they had seen wheeling through the sky earlier, swooping out of the nearby tree canopy toward the ground. "It's right here."

He removed a carefully folded piece of parchment from a pouch on his belt. Dellia did the same and unfolded hers to reveal a sprawling map rendered in perfectly repeating straight lines. Theobard marvelled at it and felt self-conscious as he revealed the collection of irregular scrawls making up his.

"Excellent," Dellia said, taking Theobard's map and focusing on the section he had added since their last lesson several days ago. "You've made real progress."

"I tried," Theobard responded with pride.

Dellia walked a little further until the curve of the wall took them out of sight of Brother Maynard, then she knelt down and spread the two maps on the ground. She arranged them so their sides touched, and Theobard could see how they came together to form an irregular circle.

"You've been keeping to the scale I gave you, right?" Dellia said, a serious look on her face.

"Yes," Theobard replied, pulling a small length of twine from his pouch. "For every twenty-five steps I took in those tunnels, I drew them this length."

"Fantastic!" Dellia said with more enthusiasm than Theobard had expected. "That means we're very close. Look, my side of the map nearly touches yours. I think we should stay focused on these tunnels in the centre. They have the best chance of meeting up."

From the moment Dellia had hatched her plan to explore the old drainage tunnels under the Sanctuary, Theobard had been both thrilled and worried. She had thought of the plan after Dak asked her to perform some maintenance in the tunnels. It was why the water clock worked again. She had been surprised at how big the tunnels were, and how they ran in every direction. There were huge machines in some of them, idle and completely rusted. Others were full of snaking pipes whose purpose she could not determine.

Once she had realised they connected to the cells in the

dormitory via their floor grates, she told Theobard about them. She said the tunnels would give them a way to meet outside of lessons, if only they could figure out how they connected together. That was when she had suggested mapping them.

Theobard was not thrilled about keeping secrets, but the thought of being alone with Dellia was irresistible. The work had been tedious, especially after a long day of his other tasks, but the tunnels had been dry, filled with a wondrous glowing lichen, and they had found nothing else in them so far; aside from the long-idle machinery, some spiders, and a few mice.

Still Theobard worried. He was sure Dak could tell he was holding things back when they talked. To be a Silent Brother was to be honest; with yourself, with others, and with Bulahl. He had been told since childhood that secrets lead to sin, but he was unable to resist Dellia's temptations. Lately, alone in his cell at night, he had contemplated Dellia and temptation a great deal.

She looked up from the map with her golden eyes toward the House of the Elders in the distance. "We're almost there," she said, the usual nonchalance on her face replaced by determination. Theobard watched her conjure an impish smile and then will her face back normal, before saying, "That's why I wrote 'tomorrow' on the brick."

Theobard was taken aback by the sudden change in her demeanour, but before he could ask about it, the hawk he had seen plunging from the tree canopy landed next to him. It let out a satisfied caw as it released a dead muskrat from its talons.

"Thanks, Greywing, but we don't want your lunch," Theobard said, annoyed it had interrupted his conversation.

"How do you do that?" Dellia said, a look of wonder crossing her face.

"Do what?" Theobard answered, puzzled, and a little frustrated the conversation was slipping away.

"Mimic animal sounds like that."

"Like what?"

"Just now," she said with obvious delight. "When the hawk landed. He cawed at you, and you answered back exactly the same way he did. Well, I mean, not exactly. Your tone was a little different, but you sounded just like a hawk for a minute."

"Oh, when I was talking to Greywing?" Theobard replied, befuddled.

"Yes, and I've seen you do it before. You've done it with mice, squirrels, and even the time we stumbled across that fox."

"I do?" Theobard said, a look of worry crossing his face.

"Yes. Don't be embarrassed. I think it's kind of cute the way you talk to animals."

"Well, they talk to me first," said Theobard, pointing at the hawk as it tore into the muskrat. "Like Greywing, here. He never shuts up. I helped him out when he was little. He fell out of his nest in the water clock, so I put him back. Now he thinks he owes me a huge debt. Always trying to make it up to me—a mouse here, a muskrat there."

Theobard noticed Dellia staring at him in disbelief. "I mean, I know I shouldn't talk to them out loud," he continued, feeling very self-conscious again. "But they don't understand the hand signs, so sometimes the only way to get them to be quiet is to say something."

"Wait." Dellia's delicate eyebrows scrunched together. "Are you saying you understand them?"

"Sure," Theobard said, wondering why Dellia was asking him such a strange question. "Don't you?"

Dellia fixed her eyes on him with intensity. It was as if she were seeing him for the first time. He wondered what was going through her mind.

"Follow me," she said, folding up her map and shoving it inside the waistband of her snug leather riding pants. "I want to show you something."

Theobard put his own map back in the pouch on his belt and walked after her. She led them further around the curving wall of the Sanctuary, away from the gatehouse. The river surrounding the Sanctuary came closer to the wall as they continued forwards, narrowing the path they walked along. Finally, the river veered off to the left, and an island appeared between them and the opposite bank, separated from the Sanctuary by a small creek.

The scrub bushes dotting the side of the path as they walked gave way to a thick undergrowth of trees, matching the dense forest of the island next to them. Dellia reached behind a thick stand of bushes butting up against the wall of the Sanctuary. "Give me a hand."

Theobard walked closer and found a large semi-hollow log stashed behind them. He grabbed his side just as Dellia grabbed hers. Together, they easily lifted it off the ground. "Help me place this across."

They stood the log on its end on the very edge of the quick-moving creek. Satisfied with its placement, Dellia instructed him to let go. The log fell, spanning the creek easily, landing with a crash.

"You've done this before?" Theobard asked.

Dellia looked sheepish for a moment and smiled slyly. "Yes, but never this easily," she said, leaping up onto the log and walking across it to the island.

As Theobard lurched across the log with awkward halting steps, he looked down into the flowing water of the creek. Directly beneath the log it became shallow, transforming its normally dark-brown water into a gold colour, not unlike Dellia's eyes. He noticed the bed of the creek rose in an almost perfect semi-circle beneath him.

When he arrived at the other side, he looked back towards the Sanctuary and thought about temptation and sin. And about safety and the comfort of sure things.

"Come on!" Dellia called to him. "It's over here."

He turned his back on the Sanctuary and followed.

Once across the log, they found themselves buried in green. The sky was only visible as dabs of blue through the canopy of trees sprawling above them. On all sides, dense shrubs and bushes lined the path, some filled with berries and others with small yellow flowers. The path they were following led away from the Sanctuary and straight towards the opposite side of the river.

After a minute of walking, the trail opened up ahead of them on a muddy riverbank. Just as it had been where they crossed the creek, there was a shallow area here, extending off into the river. After a few feet, however, it faded, and the river transformed from glimmering gold to its usual rich, dark brown.

Across the river stood the House of the Elders. This close, Theobard could see it had narrow windows, and it stood up from the shoreline several hundred feet. A set of winding stairs snaked downwards from a large front door to a rickety-looking dock on the river below, where a small rowboat, only big enough for two, was tied to the dock.

"Whose house is that?" Dellia asked, pointing across the river.

"That's the House of the Elders," he answered proudly.

"Have you ever been inside?"

"No. Only those ordained by the Abbott himself go inside."

"Why?" she asked, picking up a small stick from the ground and throwing it into the river.

"Because that house is where a faithful servant of Bulahl, who has grown too old to continue in his service, is ministered to by his fellow Brothers. He has earned his rest and lives out his days in comfort until Bulahl welcomes him into her eternal embrace," said Theobard, reciting from memory.

"So, Brother Maynard may go there one day?" Dellia replied, watching the stick float down river.

"Perhaps. Not all Brothers go there. Some die in the Sanctuary before they can make the trip."

"Have you ever seen one of your fellow Brothers cross the river?" she replied, turning her attention back to Theobard.

"Well, no," he said, looking thoughtful. "But then I only know about the House because I can see it from the window of my cell. I asked Dak about it once, when I was little."

Dellia sat on a downed tree near the edge of the river, her feet dangling in the air. A pensive look crossed her face as she stared at the slow-moving water. She began to swing her feet back and forth. Theobard searched for a place to sit but, finding none, continued to stand. Suddenly, he didn't know what to do with his hands.

"Theobard, do you know what an *amalak* is?" she asked, looking up at him.

"No," he answered, feeling confused.

"Where I'm from, every important court has an *amalak*. When a visitor comes from far away to pay a local ruler a visit, it is an *amalak* who translates his words if he can't speak the local language."

She stood suddenly and squatted down near the edge of the river.

"No important ruler could do without their *amalak*," she said, picking up a handful of stones. "They're quite valuable."

"I would imagine such men of learning would be," Theobard replied, coming closer to the edge of the river.

Dellia threw a rock far out into the river. It landed with a splash as she turned to look at him.

"They aren't all men," she said with great seriousness. " and learning has nothing to do with their talent."

She turned away and threw another rock. Theobard watched as it arched gracefully in the air. It crashed into the surface of the river, the ripples from the impact gently inching their way to shore.

Theobard stooped down and grabbed a few rocks for himself.

"If they aren't taught the languages, then how do they translate the visitors' words?" he said, launching one of his rocks into the sky.

"Because they are born knowing how," she said, skimming a flat rock several times before it sank into the brown river. "Just like you."

Theobard stopped throwing rocks.

"What are you talking about?" he said, looking toward Dellia.

"You are an *amalak*, Theobard." Dellia skimmed another rock across the surface of the languid water. "I wasn't sure until today. I thought you might be when I watched how fluently you switched between old Duarbu and Ketchi the night I arrived."

"What makes you sure now?" he asked, watching the ripples from her rock fade on the surface of the lazy water.

"The hawk," she replied. "There are stories of great *amalaks* who could talk to both humans and animals, but I'd always thought they were fairy tales."

The water of the river exploded, and the spray from it caught Theobard in the face. He heard a loud roar and stumbled backwards, rubbing his eyes. Once clear, he saw a large lizard had emerged from the river and had nearly grabbed Dellia. Theobard judged the beast to be almost as large as himself, and despite its short arms, it moved quickly across the bank of the river. It had a long tail with bony barbs, and its eyes, which rested on the top of its broad, flat head, seemed to swivel in every direction, looking for its missed prey.

Dellia leaped out of the way and scrambled towards the fallen tree she had been sitting on so carefree just moments before. The beast opened its elongated snout to reveal two rows of razor-sharp teeth. It let out a malevolent hiss before charging after her.

With a single bound, Dellia launched herself up onto the fallen tree, landing solidly on its angled trunk with both feet. Theobard was amazed by her grace and balance. As she rounded on the beast, she removed a hammer from her tool belt and took a vicious swing at it. The creature had been pulling its elongated frame up onto the tree with its stunted arms when the hammer smashed into its snout. The blow sent the beast sprawling backwards, but Dellia lost her grip on the hammer, and it spun from her hand, tumbling into the river. Fear etched itself on her face.

Theobard threw his handful of rocks at the lizard. They skittered harmlessly off its hide, alerting the creature to his presence. With a hiss, it turned away from Dellia and, with its maw wide, charged towards Theobard. Without thinking, he turned and ran into the brush.

The creature ploughed through the shrubs after him, its stunted legs furiously propelling it forwards. Theobard could hear the creature behind him, but dared not look back. As bushes and low hanging tree limbs scratched at his exposed skin, he willed himself forwards. It took every ounce of his concentration not to trip over an exposed root or rotting tree. Still, he could hear the beast closing on him.

He was brought up short by an opening in the tree canopy. Before him was a morass of soupy looking material. It seemed to be neither solid nor liquid, but a muddy mess of runny soil, dead leaves, algae, and stagnant water. He knew he would not be going through that.

He turned, desperately hoping he could backtrack and go around the quagmire before the beast was upon him, but as he did, the creature burst through the brush. Seeing him, it let loose a loud, gurgling roar and clacked its snout open and shut. Theobard knew he had only seconds before the beast pounced.

Thinking of nothing else, he backed away from the creature until he could feel the heel of his sandal start to sink in the pool of muck. The grip of the quagmire was strong, and he struggled the pull his foot free from it as the beast closed on him step by step. Theobard saw the creature squat low on its powerful legs, and he knew it was preparing to leap. Still, he struggled to free his foot from the edge of the muddy pool.

With a loud hiss, the beast bounded at him. In a panic, Theobard tried to dodge out of the way. With all the strength his thin frame could muster, he pulled on his stuck foot and the suction of the muddy pool gave way. He tumbled sideways to the ground, and it was enough for the creature to sail past him and land directly in the pool.

Theobard sprang to his feet and spun, expecting the beast to be upon him. He found it had landed several feet out in the quagmire. Despite being a creature equally at home on land or in water, none of its natural skills served it on the surface of the pond. The more the beast struggled, the faster it sank. Theobard felt guilty as he watched it slip out of sight, its panicked eyes swivelling erratically.

Dellia was standing next to him. Theobard had no idea how long she'd been there. "Not the kind of creature I would think could drown," she said in a flat tone. "I guess you learn something every day."

Theobard's heart was still pounding in his chest, and he felt like he might throw up. He was puzzled by how cool Dellia was. It was as though being attacked by a giant river lizard was something she did every day.

"Thanks for drawing it off," she said with a brisk pat on his back. "That was a close one. I owe you."

"N-no problem," Theobard stammered, unable to think of a better response, his eyes fixed on the muddy pool, desperately hoping the beast wouldn't surface.

"Well, we should get back," Dellia said, removing her hand from his back. "Our lesson is almost up. Someone will be looking for us."

Stunned, Theobard followed Dellia in silence back across the small island, toward the looming wall of the Sanctuary, lost in thought the whole way. He wondered about *amalaks* and Dellia's interest in the House of the Elders. He wondered what she'd been doing out here on her own, and why she knew how courts worked. He wondered why she wasn't terrified about nearly being eaten by a giant lizard. It occurred to him he knew very little about her.

Just as they pulled the log back across the creek and stored it behind the bushes, they saw Dak. He had come around the curve of the wall, walking with long strides and confidence, grinding the dirt and grass under his heal with each step. His face was impassive when he saw them, and Theobard had no idea what was going through is head, so he began nervously playing with the cuff of his tunic.

Dellia, Dak signed. *You are needed in the smithy. Brother*

Tanner is struggling to keep the fire hot enough to produce the alloy you asked for. Go there at once and help him.

Without responding, Dellia scrambled off and Theobard watched her go, memorising her shape and walk as she disappeared around the curve of the wall.

How are the lessons? Dak signed once she was gone.

Good, she's a fast learner, Theobard replied, his fingers moving nimbly, shame washing over him at the thought that he had not actually taught her anything that day.

She has a good teacher, he signed back, a sincere smile on his face.

Thank you. Theobard was grateful for Dak's compliment.

Dak began walking back towards the gate, and Theobard followed.

Theobard, Dak began *having Dellia here is not easy. I had to personally pledge to Abbot Emerlich that the...* His face scrunched as he searched for the right sign. *...discomfort her presence might cause in the Sanctuary would be worth what she could contribute. Bulahl is a generous but jealous god. She is the only thing that should be in your heart. Do you understand?*

Yes, Theobard signed, embarrassed his feelings for Dellia were so transparent, and ashamed he had put her before Dak, his fellow Brothers, and even Bulahl herself.

They walked on in silence for a while before Dak continued.

That said, Dak signed, a smile crossing his fleshy face *the senior Brothers and the Abbot all agree your work with Dellia, and the contributions she has made to the Brotherhood as a result, merit reward.*

Theobard could hardly believe it—his name spoken by senior Brothers! Anticipation welled up within him, and he began to nervously play with his fingers.

Which is why you will be taking over Brother Maynard's duties at the gatehouse.

It's an honour, Theobard signed back out of reflex. It dawned on him then—old Maynard's recent requests for help had been tests all along. Theobard had enjoyed working at the gatehouse, logging the different items coming in from the trade caravans and negotiating for the things the Brothers needed. Of course, he tried to do it with as few words as possible, even knowing it was not a sin to speak outside the walls, but he had to admit to himself, much like his conversations with Dellia, there was a certain thrill to the passing exchanges he had with these strangers from far-off places.

An honour earned. Brother Maynard has had nothing but great things to say about you since you started helping him.

They walked on together for a moment before Dak continued. *Do you remember how you came to the Brotherhood?*

Yes, Theobard signed, wishing he could avoid the memory.

I had hoped you'd be too young to remember, Dak replied, a gloomy look settling on his face.

Dak stopped walking. They were within a few strides of the main gate. He looked directly at Theobard, his brown eyes softening and his broad face becoming kind and loving.

Theobard, your father, mother, and all the people of your village were fools.

He placed his large hands on Theobard's narrow shoulders. Then, removing them, he signed, *You have a gift from Bulahl herself. Maynard has told me how effortlessly you understand the traders who come to our Sanctuary, how easily you speak their languages. I had hoped as much that night Dellia arrived, and I saw you speaking Ketchi. I know to you this gift is as natural as breathing, but it is extraordinary. To shun it would be to shun Bulahl. To be ashamed of it, would be to be ashamed of her.*

I understand, Theobard signed with hesitation.

Those who feared your gift, who drove you from your village because of it, will know the judgement of Bulahl.

Theobard didn't know what to say, so he stood motionless.

I am proud of you, Theobard. Dak pointed at the walls of the Sanctuary. *There are few within this place who serve it as faithfully as you. Your devotion is a credit to us both.*

Thank you, Theobard replied, his eyes moving to stare at the ground.

Dak gently grasped Theobard's chin and directed his gaze upward toward his face. *Know this. I may not be your blood, but no one aside from Bulahl could love you more.*

There was a moment of silence between them. Theobard could hear the rustle of the trees and the croak of a frog off in the distance.

I won't let you down, Theobard signed at last.

I know, Dak replied with a smile. *Now go report to Brother*

Maynard.

Dak strode off through the gate and back into the Sanctuary, his broad body shrinking into the distance with each step. Theobard watched him go, dread growing in his stomach.

Chapter Four

Theobard and Dellia embraced. Their torches lay on the ground near them, flames mingling, casting a soft golden light. Theobard thrilled at the feeling of Dellia's body against his and breathed in the deep lilac smell of her hair.

Dellia let go and got to business.

How much progress have you made? she signed, pulling her map from a pocket.

Theobard grabbed his map from the pouch on his belt and unfolded it. Unconsciously, he tugged at the collar of his black robe. It was heavier and hotter than his old tunic, but the pride he felt at wearing it made up for that. He laid the map on the dry brick floor of the tunnel next to Dellia's, the two parts making a whole. *I've only mapped another six tunnels*, he replied, feeling ashamed.

Six? Dellia signed, her fingers flashing and her face scrunching. *That's only half as many as last week.*

I know, but Dak has been keeping me busy. Between my duties at the gate, and my studies in preparation for my presentation to Bulahl, I barely have time to eat and sleep, let alone get down here to map. He looked away from her for a moment before signing again. *I'm sorry.*

We will never find the exit to these tunnels at this rate." She took a few steps away from him. *Are you still serious about this?*

Absolutely, he replied, closing the gap between them. *You know I am. It's just…* he paused, searching for the right combination of signs to appease her, and knowing there were none. *Could it wait until after my presentation? I'll have a lot more time when I'm not preparing for that.*

You're seriously considering letting them cut your voice out, aren't you?

Dellia, to serve Bulahl is a great honour. Honour doesn't come without sacrifice. All lay Brothers give up their voices. Theobard replied, proud he hadn't let his own concerns about the ceremony show.

We're leaving, Theobard. Running away, Dellia signed in a fury. *Aren't we?*

Her angry eyes bored into him, and he couldn't think of a decent response. He knew he'd never be able to explain the way his love of the Sanctuary conflicted with his love for her. Worse, he had never figured out how she felt about him. There were times she acted like they were just good friends, laughing along with him as they talked about the failings of the other monks. At other times, she touched him in a loving and familiar way, hugged him with passion, and once, he was sure, they almost kissed.

That had been on the night they had first found an exit from the tunnels. Dellia had seen moonlight glinting on a small stream of water running down the centre of the tunnel. Filled with joy, she had grabbed him and hugged him, brought her face so close that he could feel its warmth. But then she let go and ran down the curving length of the tunnel until she caught a full view of the exit and the gigantic metal crisscrossing bars that covered it. All that passion left her then.

She hadn't met him in the tunnels for two days after that. They had found three more exits since then, each the same. Theobard could tell she was growing more desperate with each one.

Dellia. Theobard tried to keep his fingers from shaking. *What if we didn't leave? What if we stayed at the Sanctuary?*

He'd finally done it. Given voice to an idea he'd had a month ago whilst lying in his cell one night. Would it really be so bad, he'd thought, to have a life together at the Sanctuary? Surely Dellia could be happy helping fix the place while he joyfully served Bulahl.

Her reaction to the idea was worse than he'd feared. She stooped down, snatched her torch from the ground and, fumbling with one hand, signed, *Fine. I'll do it myself,* then stomped off into the darkness.

Theobard ran after her, leaving his torch on the ground behind him. Desperate, he whistled loudly to get her attention. She turned on her heel and glared at him.

Dellia, he signed, dropping the map so he had both of his hands free. *Don't go.* He felt his face warm with shame. *You know I'd do anything for you.*

You do nothing for me, she replied with more clumsy one-handed signs. *You do anything for Bulahl. For Dak. They mean everything. The Sanctuary means everything. Only then me.*

She reached into the pocket of her indigo shirt and pulled out a small metal box. She threw it at him. It glinted in the light of the torches before landing at his feet. He scooped it up and stared at it. It was a beautiful, smooth metal box. The only mark on its surface, aside from the grime smeared on it when it landed on the floor, was his name etched in a flowing script.

Was going to give to you when we found a way out. Guess I won't need anymore.

Theobard felt frustration boil up. He had slept barely five hours a night over the last three months. Each night, after lights out, he removed the grate in the floor of his cell, plunged into the darkness with a single torch, painstakingly found where he'd last been on his worn map and began counting, step by step, how far he was going and in which direction. He was exhausted, and she didn't seem to notice. Or maybe she just didn't care.

Why are you so obsessed with this? he replied, putting the box in his belt pouch. *What is so bad about the Sanctuary? They treat you better than almost all the other Brothers. Don't they give you everything you ask for? All the tools? The freedom to go from place to place as you wish? They respect you as though you were a lay Brother, with ten times as much seniority, and still you want to leave. Why? Are you so selfish you need more? Are you so obsessed with your own needs you can't see what the others are doing for you? Even if we did find an exit, where would we go? You know as well as I we don't even know where the Sanctuary is, let alone how to find our way to somewhere else. Your precious freedom would leave us dead in the Dogyari within a week. How is that worth all this effort?*

He regretted signing it as soon as he finished and stood waiting for the wave of anger he knew was coming. Dellia stood silent, mulling a response. Once or twice, she started to sign, only to stop again, lost in thought. He felt a pressure rising in him, felt it enter his throat. He wanted to cough it out, to shout it out, but he knew it would not go until she responded.

"Theobard," she said finally in a tender voice. "There is so much you don't understand."

No! Theobard signed back, his fingers moving at a frantic pace. *We are not outside of the wall, speaking here is a sin!*

"I don't care," she said, jutting out her chin, a defiant look settling on her face. "I don't have the time or energy to respect your superstitions right now. I need to explain something to you."

Please, Theobard replied, grabbing her arm with one hand, and continuing to sign with the other. *It's forbidden for a reason.*

"How do you think the Sanctuary buys its supplies from the caravans?" she asked, ignoring his plea and pulling free of his grip. "Where do you think a group of men, holed up in a swamp, get the coin they need to purchase enough to feed a hundred people a day?" She winced for a moment and reflexively placed her free hand on her head.

Okay? Theobard signed, taking the torch from her hand.

"I'm fine," she continued, an obvious strain entering her voice. "I just have a bad headache all of a sudden."

Stop talking. You don't understand. Theobard signed in a panic with his single hand.

"No," she said, squinting her eyes in obvious pain. "You need to know. The Sanctuary is a prison."

He flicked his hand at her in frustration, his long fingers flapping loosely, before replying. *Just because a place has rules does not mean it's a prison. Tradition, belief, that's what makes this place special. I'm sorry you can't see that.*

"No, you idiot." She gripped both sides of her head and slowly sank to the floor. "They hold people here against their will. Lots of people. You just, ugh, don't see them."

Stop talking! he repeated. *The more you talk, the worse it will get!*

"I don't understand," she continued, rocking back and forth on the ground. "How…can…that…be?"

Because words are sin. Bulahl punishes sin in her Sanctuary.

That's crazy, Dellia replied with a clumsy, one-handed sign.

No, it's not. It's the will of Bulahl and her will is law.

Theobard could see Dellia's pain beginning to ebb, but she was still suffering. He knelt next to her, placing the torch on the worn bricks of the tunnel floor, and slowly put his arm around her. After a while, he could see she was feeling better.

What was that? she signed.

The will of Bulahl, he replied. *I am grateful your punishment was not worse.*

And that's why you don't speak? she signed, pulling away from him and standing.

Yes, to Bulahl, the human voice is foul. A sin.

But I've talked to myself here and there in my cell at night and nothing has happened before.

Bulahl is merciful, Theobard signed, grabbing the torch at his feet and standing. *She spares small sins, especially if they're far from where she lives.*

Dellia looked at him, confused. *Where does she live?*

In her temple at centre of the Sanctuary. The tower with flame on top. Theobard was unsure why Dellia didn't know that.

They walked towards where Theobard's old torch lay on the worn bricks of the tunnel floor.

I thought that was symbolic. All priests say their God lives in their temple, she signed, reaching down and picking up the torch.

No, he replied with one hand. *The temple is Bulahl's home. She dwells within. She hates the sound of human voices; it disturbs her sleep. The more she's disturbed, the more she punishes.*

Dellia brooded for a moment, her thin eyebrows scrunching together above her large golden eyes. Theobard watched as she clearly struggled with a decision. Finally, she signed, *I need to show you something,* and began walking away.

Catching up, Theobard used his free hand to reply. *Where are we going?*

The House of Elders, she signed back, continuing forward at a rapid pace.

Dellia trudged through the darkness of the tunnels with confidence, Theobard following behind, questions swirling in his mind. She navigated through the tunnels as though she had been through them a hundred times. They were just large enough for the two of them to both stand up straight and walk side by side. At first there was dried mold and algae all around, but then occasional small pools of water could be seen on the floor, and glowing lichen dotted the walls. They passed a few rusting hulks of machinery, pipes snaking away from them in every direction.

As they walked further, Theobard felt the air getting thick with moisture, and dripping stalactites began to appear on the ceiling. He felt a growing sense of guilt as they continued forwards. The House of the Elders was a sacred place. A place where only those who had sacrificed their lives for Bulahl, and the Brothers who cared for them, could go. If Dellia and he were discovered in the House, he shuddered to think of the consequences.

The tunnels dried out again, and Dellia came to a stop.

"It's okay to talk here," she said. "We are outside of the Sanctuary, under the House of the Elders."

"Dellia, what are we doing here?" Theobard said in a hushed tone. "It is forbidden to enter the House of the Elders."

"I need to show you something." She reached up to a grate in the ceiling. Standing on her tiptoes, she grabbed hold of it and pushed it free, sliding it to one side on the floor above them.

Now Theobard knew with certainty she had been here before and wondered why she had never spoken of it.

"I have to show you what this place is," she said. "Only then will you understand why we must escape."

Dellia pulled herself up and reached back to offer Theobard a hand. Out of the tunnels, Theobard found himself inside a long hallway. It had a high ceiling and was built of the same time-worn bricks as the rest of the Sanctuary. In fact, had it not lacked the ever-present curve all the buildings within the Sanctuary had, he would have thought he was back in the dormitory and that his cell was just around the corner.

"This way," Dellia said, moving away from him with purpose.

Theobard scrabbled to catch up and felt his annoyance with her fade as he watched her gracefully stride down the dark and gloomy hallway. He marvelled at her confidence and strength and wished he had an ounce as much certainty as she did. Everything Dellia did, she did completely. She never left a broken machine until it worked, never quit on a goal until she had achieved it, and never doubted herself. Theobard wondered if that same certainty applied to how she felt about him.

After walking a while, and taking enough turns so that Theobard was completely lost, she came to a stop. "This one," she said in a hushed tone.

"Why are we here?" he whispered.

"There is a man inside who can help us," she said in a low voice. "He knows where the Sanctuary is and can help us get through the

Dogyari."

"But all doors are locked at night," Theobard replied, shrugging his shoulders. "How will we get in?"

Dellia reached into the pocket of her indigo tunic and produced a key. She plunged it into the lock on the door and turned. The lock sprang open with a deep *clack*, before she placed it back in her pocket. "I made a copy of the master," she said with a mischievous smile. "Old Brother Horick never noticed it missing."

Dellia pushed the door open and stepped inside. Theobard followed.

The room was dimly lit by the glow of their torches. As Dellia quietly shut the door, Theobard could see it was well furnished. There was a large flat desk full of parchment and writing tools in front of him. To the left was a bookcase filled with worn tomes of drastically different sizes. Looking down, Theobard saw a rug lay across the centre of the room. On the far side of the room, a middle-aged man with salt-and-pepper hair sat on a four-poster bed. He was swinging his feet out from under the covers as they crossed the room toward him. He slid on a pair of slippers and gazed up at them with a look of indifference. Slowly, he removed a metal tin of matches from a small drawer in the finely carved table next to the bed. Then he lit a large candle set on the table in a simple metal holder coated in wax.

"What do you want?" he said in a gravelly voice as he stood up and took the candleholder from the table. "I've already told you I won't give it to you."

Dellia handed Theobard her torch, without so much as looking at him, and moved closer to the man. He was making his way to a plush upholstered chair sitting on the far side of the room near a large candelabra. He lit the candles one by one before sitting down.

"I've solved your problem," Dellia said with assurance. "That should be worth what I want."

Theobard saw a pair of sconces affixed to the wall near the door and placed the torches in them. As he moved back, he was struck by several benches running along the walls, each full of objects he'd never seen before: strange jars filled with preserved insects and birds; boards upon which various butterflies had been pinned; a stand featuring a large globe filled with drawings of sea monsters and different lands, each with their own name.

"I find it hard to believe you've learned Tankeshi in a month, young lady," the man said with disdain, his rheumy eyes filled with contempt.

"You're right, Ilberich. I haven't." Dellia placed her hand on the old man's shoulder before turning to point at Theobard. "But my friend here is fluent in it. He can deliver your message."

They both looked at Theobard. The man, like a hungry wolf, and Dellia, like a bazaar trader ready to haggle. Theobard could feel a dryness in his throat and swallowed quickly before nervously saying, "I will?"

"Yes, Theobard," Dellia said walking towards him. Reaching out to take his hand, she led him over to where the old man sat. "Ilberich knows how to get out of the Dogyari."

Theobard dropped Dellia's hand and stood still. "What's going on?" he asked, a look of frustration on his face. "Who is this man, and what is this message? I'm not doing anything until I know what this is all about."

There was a hard knocking sound and Theobard turned his head in the direction of the man. He was rapping his knuckles on the arm of the chair in which he sat. Once he had their attention, he stopped.

"I can see you've been playing us both for fools, young lady. This boy doesn't trust me anymore than I trust him. I think it's time you filled us both in, or this conversation is at an end."

Della sighed and Theobard could see her thinking long and hard before she continued. "This is Ilberich Bosques Grieves," she explained. "He is a master cartographer, a preeminent scholar of natural history, and a former advisor to Lord Farvald Brauerl of Eardwulf. Ilberich, please tell Theobard if you are now, or have ever been, a Silent Brother."

"Never," Ilberich replied with contempt. "I would rather die alone in the desert than become a member of this ignorant sect of joyless fanatics."

"And why are you here, Ilberich?"

"Because Lord Brauerl is a pretender to his title, and I can prove it."

"Are you here by choice?" Dellia said with a sly smile.

"Absolutely not," Ilberich replied.

"So you are a prisoner, then?"

"Of course, you knew as much when you sought me out."

Theobard looked away, puzzling over what he'd just heard. The man sitting in the chair certainly didn't look or behave like a Silent Brother. His manner and body language were haughty, and Theobard had never known a Silent Brother to have as many possessions as this man.

Theobard faced the old man directly. "If you are a threat to Lord Brauerl, why didn't he just kill you? Isn't that what lords do?" he said, straining to raise his voice above a whisper.

Ilberich let out wicked and weary laugh, Theobard winced at the sound of it. "Because, boy," he said, his rumbling voice grinding out the words. "My dear sister, the Lord's wife, intervened on my behalf. She threatened to deny him heirs if he put me to the sword. So here I am."

Dellia furrowed her brow, and a serious look settled over her face. "Ilberich would like to leave, Theobard. He has allies who can move on Lord Brauerl if the right message reached their ears. These cutthroats owe him allegiance, but, unfortunately, they only speak Tankeshi. With Brauerl gone, Ilberich can return to Eardwulf vindicated, and he can live out his days tarnishing Brauerl's reputation, while burnishing his own."

She turned her attention to Ilberich. "Is that about right?"

"More or less." Ilberich leaned forwards in his ornate armchair. "A map of this foetid swamp is a price I would gladly pay for revenge."

"And you could deliver that message, Theobard,"—Dellia looked Theobard in the eyes—"and we could use it to escape."

"Me? But I've never spoken Tankeshi," Theobard replied,

becoming annoyed.

Dellia grabbed his hand. "But you already have, many times. Half the traders who come to the Sanctuary have Tankeshi-speaking porters lugging their cargo. I've seen you give them instructions at least a dozen times. You just don't know you've done it."

Theobard thought about that for a moment. In the months since he'd taken over the gatehouse from Brother Maynard, he'd had hundreds of conversations. He'd become increasingly aware many of them were in different languages, but only because of the delightful word choices the different traders used, or turns of phrase they employed. Most of the time, to him, the conversations had been much like those he had with Dellia. It was possible, he supposed, some of them could have been in Tankeshi and he would never have known.

"Why can't he just write this message down? Then you could give it to one of the porters the next time they came around. I'm sure you could manufacture an excuse to be fixing something nearby when they arrived."

"Because Tankeshi is only a verbal language. There is no way to write it down; they don't have an alphabet." Dellia grabbed Theobard's hand, squeezing it gently. "This can work Theobard. We could be free."

"An excellent plan, Daughter of Absalom," Ilberich said. "I wish I had been patient enough for it."

Theobard watched as shock crawled across Dellia's face. Never, in all the time he had known her, had he seen her look so afraid. His hands began to sweat as a chill went down his spine.

"Yes, I know who you are," Ilberich said, ogling Dellia. "You have filled out nicely in the years since I was last at your father's court. Still, I can see in you the raven-haired girl who used to hide behind his throne."

Theobard saw Dellia consciously will away her disbelief and alarm. He could see her running through options in her mind, like she did when she was fixing some contraption she'd never seen before.

"Come on, we have to go," she said at last, dragging Theobard towards the door.

"What's your hurry?" Ilberich growled as he stood and walked after them. "You already know it's too late. The Brothers will be here before you can exit the building, so why not stay? This may be the last bit of comfort you have for a while."

"Dellia," Theobard said, his voice bubbling with anger. "What's going on?!"

"I'll explain later. We have to go." She grabbed a torch from the sconce and began to open the door.

"More like she'll lie to you later, boy, when she's had time to come up with a good story." Ilberich closed the distance between them with increasingly rapid strides. "I'm sure she has already told you more than a few. Or perhaps she's committed the greatest sin of all and convinced you she cares. Oh, that's it isn't it? How sad for you."

Ilberich let out a cruel laugh as he stepped in front of them and slammed the door shut with his large bony hand. "It took me a while to recognise you, Dellia," he said, his breath warm and sour in their faces. "I have nothing but time here, and a good memory."

"We met maybe ten years ago now at one of the grandest balls the city of Ketch has ever thrown. I believe it was some anniversary, or another of your father's triumphant returns home from the war. Absalom the Golden Giant, Hero of the Restoration. What a joke! And there you were, his beaming daughter, at his side." Ilberich reached forwards and ran his fingers through Dellia's black curly hair, eyeing her from head to toe. "Did you know your father offered me your hand that night? I regret not taking him up on it."

"Go to hell, Ilberich," Dellia said with venom.

"Go ahead and run," Ilberich said, removing his hand from the door, "but you will never leave here with your uncle. He's too old now to make the trek out of this swamp."

"Uncle?" Theobard said in disbelief. "Dellia, what is he talking about?"

"She didn't tell you that either?" Ilberich said with a laugh. "My god, boy, don't you have a suspicious bone in that spindly body of yours? That's why she's here—to free her Uncle Abraxas." He looked directly at Theobard, his red watery eyes full of wicked glee. "Let's run away together! Let's be free!" he said in a mocking voice. "Such garbage." He let out a derisive snort. "I wonder…what awful task were you doing that she had to concoct a tale to keep you going?"

Ilberich stepped away from the door and glared at Dellia. "And you! Were you so stupid to think I didn't know your uncle was here? I may not leave this cell often, but when I do, I am no fool. I gather every shred of information I can when they shuffle me through these halls. A voice calling out here, a half-seen face there. Over time, I've managed to piece together a great deal about who else is in here with me."

He took a few graceful steps back towards his chair. "I knew it was no coincidence when, less than a year after Abraxas of Ketch arrived, a handsome young woman appeared in my cell wearing boots with the image of Absalom the Golden Giant stitched into them."

Far off, down one of the stone hallways, the loud sound of a lock opening and a door creaking open, followed by footsteps, could be heard.

"We have to go!" Theobard said, pulling at Dellia in a frenzy.

Dellia didn't budge. Instead, she stepped closer to Ilberich and spoke to him with hate in her eyes. "You're a fool, Ilberich. We would have passed on your message. You could have had your revenge."

"You would have failed, child." Ilberich waved his hand dismissively. "Your insistence on taking Abraxas with you would have got you caught. There is a reason that, for centuries, the nobility have trusted the Silent Brothers with their troubles. No, much better to have the bird in the hand than the two in the bush. The Brothers will reward me greatly for ferreting you two out."

Dellia looked at Ilberich for a moment, and then Theobard watched the air rush out of her. It was like a candle being extinguished. Her shoulders slumped, her head hung down, and she looked defeated.

The sounds of footsteps grew louder.

Theobard grabbed the door handle, pulled his torch from the sconce, and clutched Dellia's hand. He yanked the door open and dragged Dellia with him out into the hallway. He could hear footfalls echoing on the bricks to his left, so he ran with Dellia into the darkness to his right, hoping the grate leading to the tunnels below was in that direction.

"Dellia!" he barked. "Which way?"

Dellia stumbled along behind him in a fog, only vaguely aware of his question.

"Come on!" he said with desperation. "We can still get away."

They turned one random corner and then another, the sound of their pounding feet mingling with those of the Brothers chasing them. Each hallway looked the same to Theobard and he wondered, in a building like this, if he might not be going in a circle, doomed to end up back where he'd begun.

Dellia yanked him to a stop with sudden authority. "This way," she said flatly.

She guided them through the inky corridors expertly. A right, then a left, then another right, before coming to a stop in front of the grate in the floor through which they'd entered.

"Theobard," she said, taking a hold of his hand, her eyes glistening with remorse. "I am so sorry."

"Dellia, it's okay. We can figure this out later."

"I do care for you," she said, barely above a whisper, "but some things are greater than ourselves."

She swung her torch at Theobard's shin with all the force she could muster. The metal guard around its top collided with his leg, sending a wave of pain shooting through his body. She shoved him backwards, and he toppled to the ground, disbelief coursing through him as he yelled out in pain.

Sprawled on the floor, he heard her lift the grate, scramble through it, and close it behind her. He lay there, unmoving; the tears brimming in his eyes, only partially due to his throbbing leg.

Behind him, he could hear the footfalls closing in, and a whistle, as one Brother called the others. Arms grabbed him roughly and hauled him from the ground. His body was slack in their grip, and his eyes fixed on the grate in the floor as they dragged him away. Heartbreak racked his thin body with convulsive sobs. Below him, somewhere, Dellia was running through those black tunnels trying to find a place to hide, trying to save herself, never giving him another thought.

Chapter Five

The air was hot and smelled of soot. Theobard opened his eyes and saw he was still in the smithy. A low fire was burning in the forge, casting a dim orange light. A large hammer lay on top of the anvil near its mouth, not far from a large bellows. To his left, a shovel was buried in a pile of inky black coal. On his right, iron ore spilled from a huge wooden bin. The lantern that had been left for him had gone out, so he stood, stretched, grabbed a wick by the forge, and lit it.

The swelling golden light of the lantern revealed an array of partially completed tools on a table across the small room from him. Rusty nails held several pieces of parchment in place over the table, and Theobard recognised Dellia's clean, precise style in the drawings. *Brother Tanner must have been making more tools for her.*

Theobard picked up one of the partially completed tools. He turned it over in his hands, wondering what it would be. It was like a hammer, only the head was pointed and slotted like a screwdriver. He thought of Dellia: tool belt on her hips, sleeves rolled up, hair tied back, and covered in sweat. Her sleek mouth screwed up into a grimace of determination as she forced some rusted and unyielding machine back to life. Then he thought of her soft hand touching his arm in a familiar way, of her self-assured laugh when he failed to understand something she'd just explained, of the way her golden eyes flashed in the sun.

He knew he had been betrayed. She had left him behind so she could escape. Once again, he replayed the moment she slipped away into the tunnel without a second glance in his mind; the grate sliding into place with the echoing clank of finality. In the seconds between her disappearance and being dragging off, he remembered, with agonising clarity, how his emotions transformed from confusion to heartbreak. How, as he lay on those cold bricks, he would rather have died than feel that pain.

He placed the tool back on the bench and wished she was there with him. He wanted that more than anything. More than being free. More than food or water. More than avoiding his impending punishment. He ached at the thought of her holding him and saying everything would be alright.

The wooden beam barring the door was raised and removed with a dull thud. Theobard thought about grabbing a tool from the workbench and using it to escape, but realised there was nowhere to go. Even if he got out of the smithy, where would he run? The Dogyari? He would be dead in days. To Dellia? He had no idea where she was. He couldn't even slip away into the tunnels below, as the smithy was the only part of the Sanctuary not connected to them.

That was when he realised. Members of the Brotherhood were usually locked in their cells before being taken to the temple for punishment. His being in the smithy was a message. They knew it all—the tunnels, the lies, Dellia's plan. They wanted him to know confession and punishment were his only options.

The door swung open and Dak walked in. There were dark circles around his eyes and a determined grimace on his face.

Come with me, Dak signed. *There is something I must show you.*

Theobard scooped up his lantern from the tabletop and scurried after him. They crossed the open courtyard of the Sanctuary, towards the dormitory.

Where going? Theobard signed, finally catching up with Dak.

The temple.

Theobard's stomach sank.

As they rounded the corner of the smithy, past the water clock, Theobard saw an orderly line of initiates, each holding a torch. They were exiting the two-story curved dormitory across the courtyard from them and marching toward the looming tower in the distance. He could make out they were wearing the simple tunic and linen pants he missed so much. From this distance, the bobbing and flickering light from their torches looked like a great writhing snake of fire.

Seeing the dormitory made him long for his room. For his lumpy bunk and the crude wooden table and chair. It made him think of how simple life had been before Dellia. Regret filled him as he walked behind Dak, and he found himself wishing he had never kept her secrets.

Dak's strides quickened, as if he were determined to reach the large gate in the square base of the tower before the initiates. As they hurried foward, Theobard caught sight of a man, dressed in a white robe, at the end of the procession. He was the only one without a torch. His hood covered his face in shadow. His hands were held in front of him, obscured from view by the long, draping cuffs of his robe. He was much taller and broader than the others and walked with a shuffling gait.

This way. Dak signed as he walked through the gate and turned right. He continued at a rapid pace through the gently curving corridor in front of them. Theobard looked behind him and saw the first initiates enter and then turn in the opposite direction away from him.

Dak slowed and Theobard nearly ran into him. The hallway had dead-ended in a set of stairs and Dak had begun ploughing up them. Theobard followed but with each step he fell behind, his heart pounding in his chest.

When Theobard caught up, he found Dak standing in a doorway at the top of the steps, looking annoyed. *Through here*, he signed, indicating his frustration with a sharp point of his finger.

Theobard followed and found himself on a balcony looking down over a enormous circular room. Without asking, Theobard made his way to the edge and looked down. He ran his hands nervously back and forth across the smooth, cool, metal railing lining the top of the waist-high stone and mortar wall. It was all that stood between him and the vast void beyond.

He began to rock back and forth on his feet.

In the circular space below, Theobard could see the initiates enter, their torches flickering in the dark. They made their way to the only other light in the room; a single torch held by Abbot Emerlich. In the many years Theobard had lived in the Sanctuary, he had only seen the abbot a dozen times. Emerlich looked vigorous, with a square jaw and long oval head, topped with black hair, greying at the temples. Like Dak, he had a high, stiff collar around his neck. It had a horizontal notch, through which you could see the angry red scar on this throat.

The initiates parted alternately to the right and left once they reached Emerlich, with the exception of the man in the white robe. He stayed resolutely in the centre. The two groups of initiates formed curving lines around a high stone pedestal directly behind the abbot. The pedestal was broad at its base and narrowed toward its top, and a set of stairs carved in its side wound around it. A thick, red velvet curtain hung from a brass rail running around the top of the tower. The rail was decorated with ornate dragonflies and lily pads.

Theobard knew, as did all the Brothers, Bulahl lay behind the curtain. It was the first truth an initiate learned when they joined. It was an unquestioned fact, like the rising and setting of the sun. Only the abbot was allowed to pierce the red veil and commune with she who lay beyond. If anyone else were to pass through that curtain, it would be the highest form of blasphemy.

Dak placed his lantern on the edge of the stone wall with a clank. Theobard looked at him.

Do you remember your initiation? he signed, his face softening.

Yes, Theobard replied. *I was so afraid.*

You should not have been. Bulahl loves all who serve her faithfully.

Still, Theobard signed. *I was small and alone. In those days, everything about the Brotherhood scared me.*

And now? Dak asked, eyebrow raised.

The Sanctuary is my home, Theobard signed with a weak, gap-toothed smile.

Then, for the good of your home, tell me where Dellia is.

There was a pause, Theobard not knowing how to answer.

Below, a bright light flared, and they both looked in its direction. A large fire near the base of the tower, roared with heat and life. Embers from the flames floated upwards like a fountain of stars, and Theobard jealously watched them ascend into the darkness.

A golden glimmer came from the metal grate in the wall directly across from him. He squinted through the dark, trying to see it better, waiting for it to happen again. It didn't.

Theobard knew Dak was waiting for an answer. With a sigh, he gave the only one he had.

I don't know where she is, he signed, hoping Dak would know he was telling the truth.

Don't lie, we found this.

Dak handed Theobard a folded piece of parchment. He didn't need to open it—after so many months spent jotting his every move on it, he knew exactly what it was.

If you help us find her, you will be welcomed back, Dak signed. Then shame crept across his face. *They may even restore me.*

Theobard looked at him and saw defeat in his frame. *What are you talking about?*

I pledged myself for you and Dellia. Your conduct was my conduct. Many of the senior Brothers thought letting her stay was a mistake. They couldn't see the advantage of having a mechanique at the Sanctuary. They didn't know why I wanted you working at the gatehouse. But I could see it. I could see how, together, the two of you would add value to the Brotherhood.

And because of me they have taken your place from you?

Yes, if Dellia isn't found, I will be sent into the Dogyari, Dak signed, looking off towards the initiates. *I was only days away from being made a prior.*

A melody began to fill the air. It came from below, somewhere in the dark. For Theobard, it brought back memories of his initiation. He recalled the Brotherhood used a large set of hollowed-out branches from the Anadaline tree to create the melody. The trees grew in clumps throughout the Dogyari, and the Brothers prized it, both for its hard bark and the food paste they could make from its pulp.

The branches were suspended by taught ropes in an upright metal frame to create a musical instrument they called the Syspici. Arranged from largest to smallest, left to right, a skilled Brother could coax a variety of rhythms and melodies from it. Theobard remembered from his initiation its song would throb and pulse along with the blood in your veins, invading your mind.

Theobard watched the abbot sign the liturgy with great, exaggerated arm movements. Behind him, in the dark, a senior Brother edged the tempo of the Syspici ever upwards. Each initiate came forwards, pledging themselves to Bulahl with quick, precise hand signs. The speed of the song increased further, its rhythm becoming more textured, and Theobard thought he saw the fire growing larger.

The abbot finished signing and ascended the stairs to the top of the tower. The melody was now a rapid-fire throb. When he reached the top, he slid behind the red curtain. Silence descended on the room.

Everyone waited, eyes fixed on the top of the tower. Then the abbot reappeared, holding a clay jar with a dragonfly on its side in both hands. As he descended, the song began again, this time slowly, its melodic notes far apart. When the abbot reached the base of the tower, he thrust the jar out in front of him. All the initiates fell to their knees, except the man dressed in white.

The music stopped again. Each initiate produced a small knife from the pouch on their belt. They held it in their right hand, looking up at the abbot with fervent eyes. The abbot approached the first initiate, pulling the jar closer to his body. He nodded his head, and the initiate cut a huge gash in his left wrist. The abbot watched as blood poured from the wound onto the worn, grey bricks of the temple floor.

Then he removed the jar's lid, reached inside, pulled forth a thick, viscous liquid and, with two fingers, smeared it on the initiate's bleeding wound. The blood stopped spattering on the ground, and Theobard knew, had he been closer, he would have seen the initiate's wrist mending itself, as though nothing had ever torn it open.

When he was completely healed, the initiate rose and signed that he would serve Bulahl with piety, fidelity, and honesty. The ceremony was then repeated for each of the remaining initiates. When finished, the abbot then gave them all one final blessing before they filed out. As they left the chamber, their torches winked out like sleepy eyes late at night.

Only the man white remained.

Theobard looked at Dak and found him staring back with intensity. *Watch,* he signed. *Learn the power of Bulahl.*

The Abbot stood below, a mere outline against the roaring fire, and stretched his hand outward towards the man in white. The man did not move. A senior Brother, dressed in a black robe, appeared from the darkness behind the abbot and walked around behind the initiate.

The abbot reached forward and pulled the chord cinched around the man's waist. With a single movement, the robe fell to the ground, leaving him naked. Theobard did not recognise the man underneath the robe. He had black skin, large round eyes, and a thick beard, smattered with grey. His hair was in long dreadlocks, bound together with a simple leather strap. His chin was bold and proud, and he stared at the abbot with defiance.

Dellia's uncle, Abraxis, Dak signed. *We know she planned to free him.*

The senior Brother dressed in black forced Abraxis to the ground with a sharp kick to the back of his knees. Once the Brother was sure Abraxis would not try to stand, he retreated back into the darkness.

The abbot moved his hands in a great sweeping arches. There was a short pause, and in the distance, a thrumming melody began. It was marshall and sinister, and made Theobard's skin crawl.

Theobard examined the naked man's face and could see the resemblance to Dellia. The shape of the chin and the corners of his mouth, the way he held himself with dignity, even as he kneeled naked on the floor. Theobard could not help but admire his body. It was heavily muscled and covered with an assortment of wicked scars. It told the story of a warrior, a man used to violence and struggle.

The melody slowed, and the abbot walked away from Abraxis. Above him, at the top of the tower, the red, velvet curtain began to part.

Theobard looked at Dak, his eyes wide and desperate.

Don't be afraid, Dak signed, his face glowing with a fanatical fervour. *For today, you will see the mighty Bulahl in all her glory as she grants Dellia's uncle the gift of redemption.*

The melody slowed further until it alternated between two low notes, like the sound of a gigantic heartbeat. It filled the room as the curtain parted further leaving Theobard feeling surrounded by its malignant vibration.

The abbot signed the word "repent" in movements so broad Theobard could easily read them from the balcony. He wondered if Abraxis understood the sign, but then saw him smile and say in a loud, deep voice, "Go to hell!"

Grabbing his head, Abraxis fell to the ground, writhing in pain. An icy expression came over the abbot's dignified face, and he drove a savage kick into Abraxis's stomach, leaving him gasping for air.

Then the curtain at the top of the tower parted fully, and Theobard saw Bulahl. She was perched on a gigantic rock in the centre of a shallow pool. Squatting, her lithe legs folded over on themselves, as though ready to spring, she was easily twice the size of a normal man.

Her long arms reached towards the edge of the pool, slowly and with grace. Theobard saw the webbing between her fingers; it was translucent in the dancing light of the roaring fire. As she crawled from the rock, and ever so carefully toward the descending stairs, Theobard saw a small fountain behind her, spraying a light shower of water. Her green and yellow skin glistened as she moved, the muscles of her supple body rippling beneath it.

Her body had the curves of a woman, with her hips and breasts swelling provocatively. As she moved, Theobard could see her delicate arms merge with her broad and powerful shoulders, but beyond her shoulders, there was no neck. Instead, above her chest, was a large, frog-like head, blending perfectly into the top of her torso. The head contained two bulbous eyes, each looking in opposite directions, and her mouth—a simple dark slit cutting her head nearly in half—began to open. As she descended the tower on all fours, horror gripped Theobard.

Abbot Emerlich looked up towards the monstrous creature slinking down the stairs with rapture, as music from the Syspici began again.

Great Bulahl, the abbot signed. *It is with joy that we offer you this sinner. May he repent and know your grace.*

The thudding beat of the melody continued, and with each boom, Bulahl crept further down the steps, crawling like a spider, and coiled to spring at any moment. Theobard felt the need to scream build within him.

When Bulahl reached the bottom, Theobard thought Abraxis looked frail and puny compared to the gaping maw of the hideous creature. Dread filled him with what would come next. He tightened his grip on the metal railing and rocked back and forth with even greater force.

Bulahl's tongue lashed out so quickly, Theobard never even saw it move. One moment, Abraxis was pushing his great ebony frame up from the floor of the temple, and the next, a gigantic, pink tendril was wrapped around him. Bulahl retracted her tongue with such force Theobard could hear a loud snap as Abraxis's spine broke.

Bulahl's slit of a mouth continued to open until it reached a horrific width. Abraxis hammered his hands on the slick, pink tongue coiled around him, but was powerless to stop Bulahl from pulling him forward as his legs dragged uselessly beneath him. Abraxis's scream was cut short as Bulahl stooped and pulled him inside her gaping maw. Saliva dripped from the edges of her bilious mouth as it closed over Abraxis, pooling on the brick floor.

Theobard could see the outline of Abraxis continue to move and struggle as he passed through the main cavity of Bulahl's body. Her chest swelled to make room for the warrior as he slid further into her, his movements only ceasing when he finally became a large bulge in her stomach.

The alternating melody stopped and Bulahl made a thunderous croaking sound. It filled every part of the chamber. Theobard could even feel it vibrating his teeth. Within that sound was meaning. Theobard heard it as clearly as if Dellia had been giving him a lecture on simple machines. The meaning was cruel and determined. He staggered back, his eyes locked on the monster below. With a single bound, Bulahl leapt back to her pool at the top of the tower. She let out another earsplitting croak as she settled back into her place on the pedestal.

Theobard recoiled. The vileness infused in that final hideous noise made his skin crawl and brought the acid from his stomach bubbling into his throat. The cruelty of Bulahl was laid bare. The intolerable wickedness of her intent, and the repulsive distain soaking her words. He felt the scaffolding of the bones holding him up crumble, and he gripped the railing for support. His knees buckled anyway, as he felt a great emptiness growing inside of him. He staggered, almost tipping over the side into the space beyond, as his faith died.

"No!" he shouted from the balcony.

The reaction was instant. The abbot, who was on his hands and knees scooping Bulahl's salvia into the dragonfly jar, glared at him with hatred and wrath.

Remove him! the abbot signed, his broad arching arms serving to carry his intent all the way to the balcony.

Dak complied, gripping Theobard's arm like a vice with one

hand, and grabbing his lantern with the other. He pulled Theobard back out into the passageway. Once in the hall, Dak released Theobard's arm and slapped him across the face, drawing blood from his lip.

You insult Bulahl? In her temple! With your voice! he signed one-handed, rage twisting his face. *I show you our God in the flesh. I give you certainty and you turn your back! Did you forget your promise?*

Dak was silent, lost in thought for a moment, and Theobard could see deep conflict on his face.

You are a failure.

But Dak, Theobard replied, his fingers moving with great speed. *Bulahl is a monster.*

Dak slapped Theobard's hands away, then clamped his hand around Theobard's arm again, dragging him down the stairs. Theobard tried to reason with Dak, but Dak would not look at him. He thought about speaking, saying out loud what was in his heart, but could not bear to suffer the resulting pain. As he bounced along behind Dak, scurrying over the broad brick courtyard of the Sanctuary, he wondered why his cry in the temple had not inflicted any pain. It was then he realised he had spoken in Bulahl's language. He felt sick at the thought of such evil sounds coming from his mouth.

Dak deposited him back in the smithy. As he exited, he turned back one last time. Theobard could see his eyes were swollen with tears, his face a mask of pain.

I had such plans for you, he signed. *We could have done great things together.*

Dak, Theobard began. *Listen to me—*

But Dak cut him off with a single slice of his hand through the air and walked out of the room. As he moved through the doorway he stopped and turned to look at Theobard. *You meant much to me once. No more.*

Then Dak shut the door, put the heavy wooden bar in place, and left Theobard to be swallowed by darkness.

Chapter Six

Time passed.

Theobard knew this because light kept creeping in. It came through the crack between the heavy door and its frame, or through the shoddy shutter that failed to blot out the room's single narrow window. It came when he lay still and silent as people entered to leave him food he didn't want and wouldn't eat. People he refused to focus on so they would pass unobserved, the incomplete darkness returning only when they left.

He could have started a fire in the forge, or even lit his lantern, but he wanted none of their light. He welcomed the darkness, craved it, wanted to be lost in a place void of intent and purpose. At night, when true darkness came, he felt as if he were spinning and tumbling through space. It was the only time things felt right.

He knew he had fallen asleep more than once because he had dreamed of Dellia and Dak. Of the lazy river surrounding the

Sanctuary, and of Graywing circling in the sky. He dreamed of Bulahl's hideous mouth swallowing everything.

Betrayal, despair, and helplessness were his only emotions. Part of him wanted things to go back the way they had been. He'd been happy serving the Brotherhood. There was simple joy in hard work and a true sense of accomplishment, even when patching bricks in the courtyard. But even if Dak forgave him, even if the Brotherhood welcomed him back with open arms, he could never forget what he'd seen. He could never forget what they served.

And then there was Dellia. While he longed for her more than ever that desire was clouded by a deep anger at her betrayal. Not just for leaving him in the House of the Elders, but for lying to him all along. It was clear to him, from the very beginning, she had an agenda, a plan, and she never once told him what it was. All along, he'd been helping her achieve some goal, and he hated her for keeping it from him—for manipulating him. But he hated himself even more for being too stupid to see what she was doing, and for trusting her at all.

Theobard heard the bar on the heavy wooden door being pushed up and set aside. It was dark out, he could tell that at least, and so far, no one had entered the room at night. Curious, he stared at the door. As it swung open, the golden glow of a lantern crawled around its edge, filling the room with a dim light. A bulky, black-robbed figure slid into the room, closing the door quietly. The figure stared at Theobard, but he couldn't make out the Brother's face, hidden as it was by the shadows cast from robe's hood. The Brother hung the lantern on a wooden peg by the door and pushed back his hood.

It was Dellia.

One lock of her curly, black hair had escaped being pulled back into a pony tail and hung in her face. Her large golden eyes glinted in the light of the lantern and her light brown skin seemed to glow in the darkness of the room. Theobard stared at her in silence, hardly believing it was true. He thought he might be dreaming. She moved towards him, a look of sorrow on her beautiful face, hand outstretched. She touched his face and the warmth of her fingers on his skin told him she was real.

Theobard, she signed, *we have to go.*

He stared at her blankly in response.

Are you okay? she signed again, her thin eyebrows arching above her luminous eyes.

I'm not leaving, he replied, his fingers moving slowly.

You have to, she signed, crouching in front of him. *You don't understand. You can't stay.*

You're right, he answered, anger flashing across his face. *I don't understand. Why don't you explain it to me for once?*

She looked away for a moment, and when she turned back, he saw real anguish on her face and tears forming in her eyes. *I'm so sorry, I never meant to hurt you.*

Well, you did, he signed with an angry flick of his fingers.

I know, she signed, sitting down next to him. He could feel her body heat, and understood for the first time he was cold and had been for a while.

I want to tell you everything, but we don't have time," she continued. *If we're going to escape, it has to be now.*

And go where? he replied, staring at her. *You know as well as I do, without a map, we will never find our way out of the Dogyari.* Then all the air went out of him and with a lazy flourish he added, *I'm better off taking my chances here.*

Theobard, the Brotherhood is going to kill you. Just like they did Abraxis. I've heard them planning it."

How do you know about Abraxis?

She looked down at the ground, her usual confidence draining from her frame. *I was there, hiding in an access tunnel. I saw what happened.*

Then you know if they wanted me dead, they would have done it already. Try another lie.

She pulled away from him.

There's no time for your self-pity. she signed quickly. *If you want to live, you have to leave this place. Dak has made a deal. What we did hurt him with the other Brothers, with the abbot. He agreed to give you to Bulahl as a sign of his loyalty.*

Like Abraxis? Theobard replied, straitening up.

Yes, she answered, looking grave.

Theobard thought it over. He could live with punishment. He could even find joy again as an initiate doing the most menial work, but he could not face Bulahl. He could not die like that. Better to drown in quicksand in the Dogyari or be bitten by a poisonous snake. Better to die of thirst and hunger than face that monster again.

Why should I believe you? he signed with a bitter look on his face. *I don't even know you.*

She let out a sigh and thought about her response before signing. *You do know me. I've been more myself the months I've been here than at any other time in my life.*

She stood and went to the door, listening for a moment before coming back. *I am Dellia, daughter of Absalom the Golden Giant, ruler of the City of Ketch and vassal to King Nashihem the First, may the Gods bless his reign. I came here to rescue my Uncle Abraxis. Ilberich was right about that. Clearly, it didn't work.*

Is that supposed to mean something to me?

No. Here, none of those things matter, but beyond the Dogyari they are very important. My father is a folk hero—more legend than man—and when I was young, I remember idolising him when he came home from one battle or another. But when the restoration happened, and Nashihem became king, he came home a different man. Broken somehow. He retreated into his tower and into his duties and became cold. Over time, he even became cruel.

What did your uncle have to do with any of that? Theobard signed. *Why was he so important to you?*

My uncle Abraxis is my father's twin. They were born only minutes apart. Some believe that gives him as much right to rule Ketch as my father. All the years my father was away adventuring, it was my uncle who kept things going in Ketch. It was my uncle who helped my mother and me. I loved him so much.

A wave of sadness passed over her. Theobard stood and put his hand on her shoulder. *I'm so sorry about what happened to him.*

I know, she replied.

Then Theobard realized that Dellia had seen him hysterical with fear and dragged off by Dak and felt ashamed.

Not me at my best, he signed, removing his hand.

Dellia looked at him with her golden eyes, they were filled with ferocity. *Never be ashamed of fear, Theobard. Fear is normal. It was brave of you to call out to that monster.*

Her compliment caused blood to rush to his face. Embarrassed, he changed the subject. *So why was your uncle here?*

Like Ilberich said, this is a place royals put loved ones who are too dangerous to have around anymore. My father grows unpopular at home, and rumours had begun that Abraxis should replace him. He struck before those rumours could become something more. He couldn't bear to kill his brother, so he had him sent here, to the Sanctuary.

Theobard still had a hard time wrapping his head around the Sanctuary being a prison. Even having seen it with his own eyes, there was still a part of him that couldn't fathom the House of the Elders holding various inconvenient royalty from beyond the Dogyari.

And you were here to get him back?

Yes. Dellia stood, confidence filling her again. *My father has to be stopped. His cruelty is out of hand, and if my uncle had returned, I know the people would have supported him.*

You thought you could free him from the Sanctuary and escape back through the Dogyari? Theobard replied.

That was my plan, but I hadn't understood how lost I would get on the way here. Each House that sends people to the Sanctuary relies on traders like the Duarbu. Only they know how to navigate the Dogyari and find this place. No House knows how to get here on its own. The traders never say, in order to keep collecting their fees. I had hoped that my uncle might remember how he got here and lead us back out, but I was never able to find his cell. When I finally came across Ilberich, after weeks of searching through the building, I thought I had a solution to all my problems, she signed, her shoulders slumping.

Now what? Nothing has changed—you still don't know where we are. What good will it do to run now?

Because right now I have a trader with a wagon waiting for us at the gate. He's Ilmari and I knew enough words in his language that when old Brother Maynard wandered off to get the ledger I was able to make a deal with him. With some coins I took from the Brotherhood's treasury, I bought us passage on his wagon out of the Dogyari. He already has half and will get the rest when he gets us out. I wish I'd thought of this plan sooner—it wouldn't have got us back to Ketch, but at least we'd have got out of the Dogyari.

Theobard thought it over. Everything Dellia said made sense, but he wasn't sure he could trust her. Her plan to free her uncle would still have left him betrayed and either on the run with them, or in trouble with Dak and the rest of the Brothers. She would still have been playing with his life to get something she wanted.

Then the image of Bulahl consuming Abraxis came into his head. Her hideous mouth extending itself wide, a relentless desire to consume radiating from it. Without Dellia, he would never have known the truth, no matter how painful. He would have spent his days serving an evil God, even eventually sacrificing his voice to the creature. He knew the truth now, and there was no way back from it.

Okay, he signed. *I'll go.*

Good, she replied, brightening up. *We have to hurry. He may decide half a payment is better than the whole thing and leave. Put this on.* She pulled another black robe out from under the one she wore, the bulk of her frame diminishing, and handed him his belt and pouch. *Thought you might need this too.*

Theobard quickly slid the robe over his thin frame, pulled the hood up over his head, and cinched the belt around his waist. *What else do you have under there?*

Wouldn't you like to know? she replied, her smile sly.

Dellia opened the door to the smithy slowly and looked in both directions before motioning him to follow. As they crept out, Theobard could see moonlight filling the courtyard, bathing it in ghostly blue-white light. Above him, the water clock *clacked*, and he saw it was approaching midnight. The torches on either side of the main gate cast their yellow light up and down the surface of the towering stone and mortar wall. They were only a short walk from the main gate, and as Theobard looked around, there was no one in sight. His heart swelled at the thought that they would make it.

Theobard followed Dellia's lead and resisted the urge to walk quickly or run for the gate. If anyone saw them, they had to make it look like they were just two Brothers headed out to help with a caravan.

They were within a few steps of the gate when Dak stepped through the opening. He looked gaunt somehow, and his eyes were shrouded in the black circles of one who has not slept well.

I hoped you would come for him, he signed to Dellia with a wicked smile. *I thought you were at least decent enough to help him escape his fate.*

From behind Dak stepped three Brothers of the night patrol, their curved swords glinting in the light of the torches affixed to the gate. Theobard took a step back as they pulled their swords, the sound of the metal blades grinding against their sheaths echoing across the courtyard.

Theobard looked at Dellia and knew the expression on her face. She was thinking things over —running through every angle— trying to find a way out of the situation. But Theobard knew she wouldn't find any. There was no way past Dak and the three Brothers. And even if there was, they would never get to the Ilmari wagon before they were caught from behind and dragged back inside.

Then Dellia lashed out.

There was a hammer in her hand and Theobard realised under her bulky robe she was still wearing her tool belt. She slammed it into Dak's arm and there was a loud crunching sound. Dak would have screamed if he still could.

She followed up her attack by crouching down. One of the other Brothers took a swing at her, his sword whistling through the air. She kicked out sideways and knocked his feet out from under him. He slammed face-first into the ground.

"Go!" she yelled, and Theobard saw her wince as she said it.

He ran toward the gate but found his way blocked. There were still two Brothers left, and while one moved to engage Dellia, the other kept himself firmly trained on Theobard.

Theobard looked around desperately for anything that would help. The courtyard was mostly empty, except for the wheelbarrow he used when patching its damaged bricks. He leapt towards it, just as the Brother swung his curved blade at him. The blade nicked the sleeve of his robe, leaving a long gash.

Having reached the wheelbarrow, he looked inside. It was full of sand and a few broken bricks. He grabbed a handful of debris and turned around. The Brother was charging at him, his face contorted in anger, and Theobard hurled the sand at his face. It collided with the Brother's wide eyes and he dropped his sword, clawing at his face, his mouth agape in a silent scream.

Theobard reached into the wheelbarrow again, grabbing a large brick fragment, and threw it at the Brother. It caught him square in the face and he fell to the ground, blood rocketing from his broken nose.

Theobard looked over at Dellia. She had been driven back a few feet from the gateway and was parrying slashing sword blows from the remaining Brother with her hammer. Theobard realised then what a skilled fighter she was as he watched her fluidly disarm the Brother and smash his jaw with the hammer.

He turned and ran for the gate. When he reached it, he looked back, expecting Dellia to be behind him. Instead, he saw her being held by Dak, who had lurched back to his feet and grabbed her robe with his good arm. She was struggling to turn and face him when she locked eyes with Theobard.

"Go!" she screamed, and Theobard saw pain shoot through her body. "I'll catch up."

Theobard bolted around the corner and saw, in the distance, old brother Maynard arguing with the Ilmari trader, who was dressed in a flowing robe with a wide sloping hat. The trader spotted Theobard, and, with an ungracious shove, sent Brother Maynard sprawling to the ground before jumping into the seat of his covered wagon.

Theobard hopped up into the back of the wagon and heard a loud clang echo through the night behind him. He spun around to find Dellia and saw the portcullis closed, its gleaming façade shining in the moonlight.

On the other side of it, Dellia was removing a small stick from the gate's release mechanism. Behind her, the Brothers of the night patrol were getting to their feet as Dak lay rocking back and forth on the ground.

"No!" Theobard screamed as he watched the Brothers strip her of her hammer and knock her to the ground, where she landed with a rough bounce.

Theobard moved to the edge of the wagon, preparing to jump from it, when it lurched forward. He lost his balance and stumbled backward, striking his head on the wooden frame holding the wagon's canopy in place. He saw stars shoot before his eyes and his vision began to grow dark, like there was a tunnel closing in around him.

Desperate, he looked back to the gate, already growing smaller as the wagon sped away into the Dogyari, and saw Dellia's golden eyes locked on him, even as she was dragged away.

Then he fell backwards and passed out.

Chapter Seven

I'll give you two kroners for it," Theobard said, flashing his gap-toothed smile. "It's the best deal you'll get anywhere in the Matori Bazaar."

"You know, as well as I," replied the burly trader, "a bracelet as fine as this is worth twice that."

"It *is* a fine piece of jewellery," Theobard said, rotating it around in his hand and pointing at a small, engraved ram. "But it also bears Lord Bunka's seal. It loses some value for being stolen."

The burly trader grumbled but took the kroners and went on his way.

"Theobard," Mansell said, walking up behind him in the stall. "I thought you might want to see this."

Mansell handed Theobard a piece of parchment rolled up and tied with a bit of twine. He smiled and Theobard could see, even under Mansell's scraggly grey beard, the wrinkles lining his weathered face bunch as a result.

Theobard's hands shook slightly with anticipation as undid the twine. He suspected what it was, even before he unrolled it, and laid it flat on the table fronting the stall. It was a map, and this one had the entire Dogyari drawn on it. It was a beautiful piece of work with fine drawings of the Pena Mountains to the East, and glimmering Ketch to the west. Roads snaked across the map, connecting distant lands, and small sketches of monstrous figures indicated those places the map maker didn't know well. His eyes took in every detail, but after a few moments, he looked up at Mansell with disappointment.

"It is a fine map," Theobard said. "The best one you've found yet but—"

"It's not on there, is it?" Mansel said, putting a hand on Theobard's shoulder.

"No."

Mansell took the map, rolled it up, retied the twine, and walked across his small stall to the rear. He placed it in a wicker bin with the other maps and odds pieces of loose art. Theobard watched him do it and felt his disappointment melt away, replaced with gratitude, when he thought about how lucky he was Mansell had found him a year ago.

Theobard let the noise of the bustling bazaar fill his ears and watched as people from across the known world shuffled past. A large hand-painted sign reading Mansell's Marvels hung just below the top of the table, and those who frequented the Matori Bazaar knew you could get grain anywhere, but if you really wanted something special, you came to Mansell.

His tiny, unassuming stall, with its faded but colourful peaked roof, was where wonder was bought and sold. Anyone with anything odd brought it to Mansell. Anyone looking for the unusual came and bought it from him. "My business survives by taste alone," Mansell had told him early on. "It's my responsibility to know not what my customer wants, but to know what he doesn't yet know he wants."

Mansell had found Theobard wandering around the bazaar, penniless and hungry. After passing out in the Ilmari trader's wagon, he'd woken in a side alley off the bazaar. Theobard had no idea how he'd got there. He suspected the Ilmari trader, arriving in Matori with an unconscious body and half the money he had hoped for, had cut his losses and pitched Theobard into the alley like an old, threadbare rug.

With nothing but his clothes, and after a long day of looking for work, he had resorted to begging at the bazaar. That was when Mansell had first seen him. When Mansell told the story, he would often say he hadn't paid Theobard the slightest bit of attention, and thought him just another beggar at the bazaar. But he'd watched as Theobard asked for kroners in six different languages, as though he was a native speaker. Fascinated, Mansell continued to observe, noticing how Theobard might approach a person with one language, switching to the correct one as soon as they spoke, sometimes in mid-appeal.

Of course, Mansell had heard of an *amalak* before but, as he was a merchant and not nobility, he had never seen one in person, let alone one hungry and asking for a handout. Understanding Theobard's value, he convinced him to come back to his home, cleaned him up, fed him, and offered him a job working at the stall. Theobard had been there ever since.

"Mansell's Marvels!" Theobard called out to the passing crowd. "Come find what you didn't know you were missing!"

Mansell joined him at the table. He pulled up the stool he kept under the table for when his old knees howled with age and sat down with a huff.

"I'm sorry that wasn't what you were looking for, Theobard," the old man said. "One of these days, I'm sure we'll find it."

As soon as he was able, Theobard had told Mansell about Dellia and the Sanctuary. At first, he had asked him on a daily basis if he might know how to find the Sanctuary, if he knew anyone who might know, if there was anywhere he could search for its location. Mansell, regrettably, had said no to all Theobard's inquiries.

Still, he kept an eye out for anything new coming through the bazaar that might be what Theobard was looking for. Mansell had been around long enough that with a word he could let the whole place know when he was interested in paying for a particular item. Sooner or later, what he was looking for would find its way to him.

Mansell could see Theobard was lost in thought. He'd been quiet when he'd first found him, reluctant to talk at all, but through months of working at the stall, Mansell had watched him bloom. He had a real talent for conversation and seemed to genuinely enjoy talking with all the people who passed through Matori.

Not much more than a hundred mud huts, Matori had an outsized bazaar because of its location at a major crossroads. It meant that, on top of being a place where farmers brought their goods to market, traders going to and from any major city in the kingdom had to pass through sooner or later. That made life easy, with abundant cheap food, and more customers than most merchants had any right to.

Despite this, Mansell knew Theobard was unhappy. He put on a brave face, and his natural tendency toward being positive kept him from outright despair, but he could see past the mask most days, to the hurt beneath.

He knew Theobard nursed the pain of one who waited. One who pined for something that could not be. Theobard hoped to find a map that would lead him back to the Sanctuary, even though he had no plan for rescuing Dellia even if he managed to get there. And, more than that, Theobard hoped Dellia would emerge from the throngs pulsing through the bazaar and find him—he knew both things were improbable, but that was the problem with hope; it persisted.

Mansell understood, from years of living, how existing in a state of hope, of yearning, kept a man frozen in place. Never allowing him to grow or change. Never allowing him to become who he really was. Life was about moving forward, Mansell believed, and watching Theobard broke his heart.

Mansell gave Theobard a nudge with his elbow. "Hey," he said with his smooth baritone voice, "did you see a team of royal alchemists arrived in town last night?"

"Oh?" replied Theobard, continuing to stare absently at the passing crowd.

"They are on their way back to Belvaro and the king's court."

"That's interesting," Theobard said, paying little attention.

"I heard they lost half their porters in the Pena Mountains, attacked by some kind of snow beast."

"Sounds terrible." Theobard yawned, glazed eyes scanning the people walking past.

"I hear they are desperately looking for replacements."

"Well, good luck," Theobard said. "It's hard to find anyone in this town who needs work these days. Between the trade here at the bazaar, and how easy it is to join a caravan, all they are likely to find are old men and boys running away from home."

Mansell stared at him for a moment, amazed at how thick headed he could be.

"Theobard," he said, slowly. "I think, when those alchemists leave tomorrow, you should go with them."

That got his attention. Theobard turned from the passing crowd and looked at Mansell as though seeing him for the first time that day. "Are you telling me to leave?" he asked, looking both hurt and frightened.

"No, no, no," said Mansell, touching Theobard's arm in a gentle, reassuring way. "It's just—a young man like you shouldn't live his life in this little stall, in this little town in the middle of nowhere."

"But I like it here. I don't want to go anywhere else."

"Theobard, take it from one who knows, it's better to live on that side of the table than this one."

Theobard looked at the crowd again. He watched it surge through the bazaar and saw people of every size, shape and form, each with purpose. He knew some of them were desperate, and some fortunate.

Some were just there buying routine supplies, but others were engaged in adventures he could only guess at.

"I know you want to find Dellia," Mansell said with his low, flowing voice. "But have you ever considered she isn't coming, or doesn't want to be found?"

"No!" Theobard practically shouted. "That's not true. I know she's out there, and if it wasn't for her, who knows where I'd be. I'm not giving up on her."

"But what if she's given up on you? Are you really willing to spend the best years of your life waiting for her? From what you've told me, I'm not sure she would do the same."

Mansell knew he had pushed too far, but he felt he had to tell Theobard the truth. He could see he'd hurt Theobard's feelings and watched as the young man turned away without making a sound, tugging at the cuff of his shirt sleeve.

"Here," he said, putting a beat-up belt and worn leather pouch on the table. "I was cleaning out the house this weekend, and I found this. I nearly forgot the night I brought you home, I made you get rid of your filthy clothes. This must have ended up under my bed."

Theobard looked at it with intensity, recognizing his old belt right away. He could remember how it felt when it held his black robe in place, could remember the soft touch of Dellia's hand when she passed it to him the night he'd escaped. Gently, he picked it up.

Mansell wandered off to the back of the stall and pretended to do some inventory. He thought it best to let Theobard consider what he'd said alone. Theobard opened the pouch and looked inside. It was full of odds and ends. His measuring string, a bit of parchment, some drawing charcoal, and a metal box. Theobard removed the metal box and saw his name on it. He remembered Dellia giving it to him in the tunnels under the Sanctuary.

He saw a line run all the way around the metal box, indicating that it could be opened. On one side of it were some recessed hinges, and on the other, a small metal button set flush. He pushed the button and felt the top of the box pop open. He lifted the lid and, as he did, its interior—a collection of finely crafted metal pieces and moving gears—unfolded into the shape of a glittering hawk. It was in mid-flight, as though soaring through the air. It was full of intricate details, from the pattern of feathers on its wings to the gentle curve of its fierce talons.

Along the right-hand side of the hawk there was an unfurling paper scroll fluttering in an invisible wind. On it, etched in Dellia's perfect flowing script, were the words "Fly Free!" and, below that "Love, Dellia."

Tears filled his eyes, and he closed the box. He knew Mansell was right; if Dellia had escaped, and was coming to find him, she would have done it already. He also knew he would never find her in the Dogyari, let alone free her from the Sanctuary. It dawned on him then she had given him a great gift he could never repay. She had given him the world, whether he wanted it or not, and to waste that would be to waste her sacrifice.

He put the box in his pocket and went back to calling out to the crowd. He attracted many customers that day. He bought and sold many wondrous items and made a healthy profit. When the day was over, he thought to himself that alchemists from the royal court would be quite the thing to see and decided to walk over to the boarding house where they were staying. Maybe they would know something about where the Sanctuary was.

The next day, Mansell arrived early to open his stall. He found a note on the table in Theobard's childish handwriting. He opened the note, and it read:

"I decided to take your advice. I'm off to Belvaro. I will never forget you or how you helped me when I needed it. Your friend, Theobard."

Mansell closed the note and put it in his pocket, a satisfied smile crossing his face at the thought that he'd helped yet another customer find something they hadn't known they were looking for.

𝔐𝔦𝔠𝔥𝔞𝔢𝔩 𝔍. 𝔖𝔱𝔦𝔢𝔥𝔩

MICHAEL J. STIEHL writes speculative fiction of all varieties, from fantasy to horror to weird westerns. Frankly, there is just no telling what he'll put on the page next.

Michael is a full-time staff member, and adjunct faculty, at the University of Chicago. With a lifelong passion for fiction, in particular horror, comics, adventure, and science fiction, he is thrilled to be pivoting away from academic publications and towards the kind of fiction that has always inspired him.

Michael lives in the Chicago suburbs with his wife, two kids, and their very silly poodle, Jack. When not writing fiction, Michael spends his time riding bikes, camping, reading books, obsessively listening to music, and playing D&D with his friends. In short, he hasn't changed at all since junior high.

Michael's work has previously appeared in the Rogue Blades Entertainment anthologies, *Reach for the Sky*, and *No Ordinary Mortals*. He has also been featured on the Night Shift Radio Story Tellers series.

Bibliography

NO ORDINARY MORTALS, Rogue Blades Entertainment, 2022

NOM NOM, Black Hare Press, 2022

REACH FOR THE SKY: A HEROIC ANTHOLOGY OF THE WILD & WEIRD WEST, Rogue Blades Entertainment, 2020

TWIST OF CAIN, Nightshift Radio Storyteller Podcast Print Edition, 2021

Connect

Facebook: @michael.stiehl

Black Hare Press

BLACK HARE PRESS is a small, independent publisher based in Melbourne, Australia. Founded in 2018, our aim has always been to champion emerging authors from all around the globe and offer opportunities for them to participate in speculative fiction and horror short story anthologies.

Connect: linktr.ee/blackharepress

Joe Oppenheimer

115

Clown Diary – Appendix 7

by Joe Oppenheimer

Joe Oppenheimer

PREFACE

Three days after the tragic circus fire of May 4th, 2027, in Alta Vista, VA, Officer Roben Klarenvelt, a volunteer member of the Campbell County Forensic Cleanup Crew, found these pages. They had blown about on the fair grounds at the state capital. We presume that other pages were burned and lost. Judging by format and handwriting, the pages are from the same diary, and we present them as such. Forensics has not been able to determine who the author is, and what his fate might have been in the fire.

With each entry the author drew a vertical line on one of the pages and included a poem to the right of the line. Mrs. Helenor Plimpton, our secretary, was kind enough to transcribe the pages and to place the poems with the entries, in a separate 'box.' The typescript of the original collated pages and the transcription are herewith handed in as Appendix 7 to our final report of the fire. The originals are contained in the secondary files concerning the properties judged to be abandoned at the scene of the fire. Those files are maintained in the County Archives by the Campbell County Board of Records in Rustburg.

This appendix ends our legal obligation to the Campbell County Executive in accordance with County Law MCPL3212, section B.

Lt Eugene Skaarfeld, OIC, OCFCC

Campbell County Sheriff's Office

87 Courthouse Ln, Rustburg, VA 24588

August 18th, 2027